A Love to Die for

by Joseph Seechack

© Copyright 2024 Joseph Seechack

ISBN 979-8-88824-198-1

All rights reserved. No part of this publication may be reproduced, stored in a retrieval system, or transmitted in any form or by any means—electronic, mechanical, photocopy, recording, or any other—except for brief quotations in printed reviews, without the prior written permission of the author.

This is a work of fiction. All the characters in this book are fictitious, and any resemblance to actual persons, living or dead, is purely coincidental. The names, incidents, dialogue, and opinions expressed are products of the author's imagination and are not to be construed as real.

Published by

3705 Shore Drive
Virginia Beach, VA 23455
800-435-4811
www.koehlerbooks.com

A LOVE
TO DIE FOR

JOSEPH SEECHACK

VIRGINIA BEACH
CAPE CHARLES

PROLOGUE

Ron and Grace Butler had the kind of love that inspired the greatest poems, love stories, and love songs: a deep, pure, limitless love. Everyone saw their incredible magic. Maybe it was the way they played and joked with each other. Perhaps it was the glow surrounding them, exuding a warmth that people loved to bask in.

Love shows itself in sacrifices made, and Ron and Grace would do absolutely anything for each other and their children, anything. You might wonder, with the love they shared, what could possibly go wrong. Alas, the shining brilliance of their lives together made the events that follow all the more tragic.

This is Grace's tortuous ordeal—as well as her triumph.

CHAPTER 1

GRACE'S DOCTOR'S APPOINTMENT

Grace Butler had an all-important doctor's appointment with a specialist that morning. She hadn't slept well the night before. She tossed and turned over a portentous feeling of dread. Women know that feeling intuitively, and it was very familiar to her. Something bad was going to happen.

Twenty minutes before the alarm clock went off, Grace's husband, Ron, was already awake. He wanted to let her sleep as long as she could, then spring into action the moment the alarm went off to help his lovely bride prepare for her appointment.

When the relentless alarm finally rang, their day began with Ron's smiling face and twenty-four morning kisses, like two dozen roses, for his queen—just like every day. Now he could go downstairs and start making breakfast. He wanted to make Grace's favorite, blueberry pancakes and breakfast sausages, to give the woman he loved the best possible start to the morning.

Grace lay in bed for a while longer, enjoying her stretch, trying to transition into being fully awake. She contemplated the feeling of dread and hoped it was merely the aftershock of a bad dream. Meanwhile, the minutes ticked by. Her appointment was at eleven. But the bed was far too comfortable, so she overruled the clock radio and tried for a few more winks.

Unfortunately, Ron refused to let her sleep longer. He bounded upstairs to check on his beautiful bride.

"Wake up, beautiful. I love you."

Grace stretched again and said, "Five more minutes, Ma."

Ron laughed and snuggled some of her sleep away.

"You know, babe, it is such an incredible blessing from God to wake up next to you every morning. God has been so very generous with both of us. We have each other and always will. Thank you, Jesus! Now, get your cute little rear into gear."

"Five more minutes, Ma," Grace repeated with a giggle.

"I heard you, babe: 'Five more kisses, Ma' coming right up." And Ron kissed her four times on the mouth and once on her nose.

"Ron, why do you kiss me on the nose?"

"Well, your delicious lips get all the attention. Your nose is just sitting there, feeling lonely, out of place, ignored, and left out. I wanted your nose to feel like part of the family."

"You know you're *nuts*, Ron!"

"Absolutely certifiable! I'm nuts for you. I'm sure that if you had gotten just a few more signatures on a petition, I would be committed to Bellevue or some other mental asylum. But too late! I'm already committed to you, my love, for life. Now, Grace dear, put your cute little dancing cheeks in the shower, or I'll give you a hard slap right on your drumsticks."

Grace said, "Oh, but you wouldn't, Ron."

"Oh, but I would. Right there on your cute little drumsticks."

Grace wouldn't let him accompany her to her doctor's appointment because he had been sick, and according to the weather reports, the rain in Big Sur would continue for the next few days. Ron had been feeling weak and tired from all the coughing, sneezing, and sleepless nights, and she worried too much about his health because he didn't worry enough—not just about the severe cold but about his heart problems too.

So, Ron put on the kitchen radio. *Maybe they'll surprise me this morning and play something really good, like Judy Collins or Laura*

Nyro. He shook his head at himself. *Nah, they'll play whatever it takes to sell commercials.* He cooked while Grace showered and got dressed. As he bustled around the kitchen, he thought about the first time he and Grace met. It was at a restaurant. Ron glanced at Grace, and then she glanced at him. They both took a moment to see if their glances were half-full or half-empty. They both knew that their glances were full and overflowing

Ron walked over and introduced himself. He said, "I couldn't help but notice you noticing me. My name is Ron Butler. Your name must be Beautiful." The rest is one of love's greatest hits. If love had a Mount Rushmore, Ron and Grace would be on it.

Back in the present, the smells of Ron's cooking attracted the attention of Grace's cat, Chief Inspector Moonbeam, who was looking for something, anything to eat. If Grace and Ron were willing to eat it, Moonbeam was willing to sniff it—and might consider shoving it on the floor to eat it herself.

Ron yelled to Grace, "Hey, honey, breakfast is almost ready. Get it while it's hot."

Grace barely heard him from the shower but correctly assumed that an announcement was being made. He didn't at all hear her answer, "Be right there."

The radio kept talking about the heavy rains. Ron didn't want Grace to go out in the rain, most especially to drive in the rain, but it would be a mortal sin to break this appointment.

Dressed and ready for breakfast, Grace announced, "Oh, blueberry pancakes, my favorite. Thank you, dear" with a smile and a kiss. Chief Inspector Moonbeam jumped from the top of a kitchen cabinet to closely examine the breakfast menu. Maybe they were serving something she liked.

Ron told Grace about a fourth day of torrential rain and more flooding in the forecast.

"I know, honey," Grace said. "But what can I do? You know how it is with appointments with a specialist. Just make sure you get that Thundershirt on Moonbeam. You know how the thunder and lightning scares her to death."

Ron answered, "Okay, honey, I'll take care of Moonbeam."

"You promise?" Grace asked.

"Yes, dear, thank you, dear. I promise to take care of the one true love of your life, your 'significant other,' the one closest to your heart, your little darling Moonbeam."

After breakfast, they had a long, lingering, loving hug and a passionate kiss goodbye before Grace headed out to her car. Ron wouldn't let her go.

He said, "I'm afraid that if I let you go, Grace, I will fall out of heaven and never see you again."

"Oh, Ron, you say the most romantic things."

Ron kissed the top of Grace's hand and lovingly rubbed it against his heart three times to make it official and permanent.

The heavy Big Sur Pacific rain had already started again. Beneath her umbrella and under Ron's loving, protective gaze, Grace carefully walked to her car. Ron watched her drive away, whispering a quiet prayer for her safe return.

Ron went back to the kitchen to clean up the breakfast dishes. He then relaxed on the living room couch in front of the news. *Thank God for TVs!* he thought. *After all, without TVs, how would you know where to put the couch?*

During a commercial break, Ron checked his email and saw messages from the kids. One was from their son, Ryder. The other was from their daughter, Melody. Fraternal twins, Ryder had been named to reflect Ron's profession as a writer, and Melody's name was inspired by Grace's former profession as a high school music teacher.

Ryder was attending USC in Los Angeles. He was majoring in literature to pursue his goal of becoming a writer, like his father, or to maybe someday teach writing. Brilliant and bordering on cerebral, he often spoke very quickly. Most people thought he was from New York City or worse, but his mouth was just trying to keep up with his mind.

Melody was majoring in medicine at UCLA with the goal of becoming a doctor. She was quite beautiful, and although she was demure, she unleashed the biggest belly laughs at things Ryder would say, and you couldn't help but laugh along with her.

Both emails were very similar, thanking Mom and Dad for a wonderful Easter holiday.

Between his severe cold and the "tedium in the medium" coming from the TV, Ron drifted off to sleep, forgetting his promise to Grace.

The sound of a thunderclap shocked him awake, followed by the realization that he should have put the Thundershirt on Moonbeam right after Grace left. Concerned about the cat, Ron called for her four times and looked everywhere at least twice. He didn't know how the cat could have gotten out, but he couldn't find her.

If only Grace had gotten a dog like he wanted, he wouldn't have this problem. Dogs are loyal. They're man's best friend for a reason. But a cat . . . cats must have an answering service or a secretary or something. Just leave a message, and the cat may or may not get back to you, eventually. But only if the cat is in a very good mood, and only if you're incredibly lucky.

"Damn arrogant cat!" he burst out. "Doesn't she know that I have to go out in the heavy rain and the howling, freezing wind and all the flooding to look for her? Maybe she went out shopping or something. Everyone knows that when the going gets tough, the tough go shopping. Or maybe she went out for a pizza with catnip on it instead of oregano. Who knows?"

Ron just knew that the cat had escaped on his watch, making it his fault, his responsibility. He had to do something.

He couldn't call the missing pussycat line. Moonbeam had to be gone at least forty-eight hours for them to act. He couldn't call the fire department. He didn't know what tree the cat might be stuck in. The cat might be leaping through all the trees in the forest, one at a time, like Goldilocks. You know, the first one was too wooden. The second one was too soft. But the rest of the trees in the forest were just right. Besides, looking for a cat in a forest would give him a cramp in his neck. *Maybe it's better to try somewhere else.*

"Hmm! Where would a diabolical, free-spirited, psy-cat-ic luna-cat escape to in order to make my life all the more miserable, especially on this fourth day of endless rain?"

Ron was a somewhat intelligent guy, on a good day. He should be able to reason this out. So, he mentally morphed into a cat, to see things from Moonbeam's perspective. Sort of like a cat profiler. But Ron was too big and fat to be small and cuddly like the cat.

Well, Ron thought, *it's raining pretty damn hard out here. You might say it's "raining cats and dogs." And cats don't like to get wet. Where could I find shelter for myself? Maybe the cat would go to the same location.*

Ron bundled up nice and warm and headed out with his flashlight.

Trudging around in the freezing-cold rain, he swiftly became soaked *past* the skin, down to his internal organs. *We should change the cat's name from Moonbeam to Amelia Earhart.* That would be a more appropriate name for a missing female cat. Of course, Amelia Earhart was never officially found, so maybe not.

It started to rain even harder, and the wind blew quite strongly, whipping the trees back and forth, making this adventure into the aquatic unknown all the more special. *Thank you, Moonbeam.*

He soon realized that the rain would soak the ground and drain into the creek through the new galvanized drainpipe the county had started to put in to avoid flooding problems. *The drainpipe! Why didn't I think of that sooner?*

At least now he had a plan. It probably wouldn't work; none of his plans worked—kinda like a modern-day Ralph Kramden from *The Honeymooners*. But it was the best he could think of under the liquid circumstances. If nothing else, at least he could protect himself from the rain while the walking pneumonia worked a little longer and harder on finishing him off once and for all.

He sloshed through the forest and over to the creek. With the help of his large lantern flashlight, Ron followed the flow of rainwater to the drainpipe and climbed in. It wasn't elegant, but he was out of the rain.

Catching his breath, he hoped that this drainpipe would lead him to the cat; he would get the galvanized shaft if not. But to his amazement, he heard a meow. *Moonbeam?*

"I tawt I heard a putty tat."

To Ron, the meow sounded like "So, what took you so long, fat boy? Don't you have enough sense to get out of the rain?" This arrogant cat had no respect for the fat fool who fed her every day. As Dollar-Bill Shakespeare never wrote, "Sharper than a serpent's tooth is the ungrateful cat."

At least Ron had found Moonbeam. Still, there was a problem. The drainpipe was fairly small, and Ron was very large. He couldn't turn around. So he backed out in the most dignified way possible to remove his heavy, waterlogged coat, and then it was his happy privilege to climb back in and crawl toward Moonbeam, who was meowing again.

The large flashlight wasn't doing him much good, so he left it with his sodden coat just inside the opening of the drainpipe.

"Oh, how I love her so. Yeah, right!" *Wait till I get my hands on that fleabag.* He contemplated committing "felineous assault" on the creature. Ron was out in the howling wind and the endless, freezing rain not because he loved the cat but because he loved Grace. And he didn't want to see Grace hurt, which she certainly would be if she lost her furry, four-legged child. The fact that the cat ran away on his watch would make it all the more painful and might harm their marriage significantly.

He had to find Moonbeam, regardless of the cost!

Ron wasn't sure how deep inside the drainpipe the cat had traveled and how far he had to follow. A cat shouldn't have to go very far to escape the rain. But who knows, with cats? Maybe curiosity and fear made her go deeper—or maybe hearing Ron coming into the drainpipe did.

Ron followed the meowing on his soaking-wet belly, trying to talk the cat into coming to him. But to no avail. Now Ron heard only the heavy rain on the drainpipe and the whirling winds blowing.

CHAPTER 2

THE ROUND COFFIN

Narrowly focused on rescuing Moonbeam, Ron wasn't thinking of his own safety. He wasn't considering how far he had traveled into the pipe. Every time he called out to Moonbeam, he thought he heard a meow in response. And that drove him deeper and deeper. Ron was oblivious to the danger—a clear case of tunnel vision inside this galvanized tunnel.

In the very dim light of a drainpipe on a stormy day, even the shadows had shadows. This level of darkness didn't exactly illuminate his situation. In addition to the obvious, he started to have problems breathing, partly due to exertion from squeezing into such tight quarters. But mostly it was his weight. Ron was morbidly obese, hence the heart condition.

They say, "Curiosity killed the cat." But Ron would likely end up as Moonbeam's collateral damage. Who knew what else used this pipe as a shortcut to somewhere? Maybe the animals were at work now, but they might be heading home soon in an animal rush hour. And animals see far better in the dark than humans and would not be used to the obstruction of a human body. How would they react? Would the animals see him as a danger to be avoided or as a threat to be confronted? Either way, Ron was fresh meat, a crawling feast.

In the almost total darkness, he couldn't see where his next breath was coming from. The meowing stopped. Was he getting closer to Moonbeam, or did she leave the other end of the drainpipe? *If she got out, maybe I can too. Maybe, in all this darkness, there's a light at the other end of the tunnel.* And maybe Moonbeam would be there, laughing at him.

"Damn arrogant cat!"

He didn't know if his eyes were playing tricks on him, but he thought he saw a glimmer of light ahead. *Just another few feet*, he promised himself, *and I'll be free*. He pressed on, soon hearing the howling of the wind, which had gotten much more severe. But the breeze on his cheek and the fresh air that came with it felt nice.

Beyond exhausted, he stopped to rest. He rested his head on his forearms to keep his mouth out of the rainwater. He just needed a few minutes to collect himself before striving for the finish line, and home, and Grace.

Unplanned, unexpected, he drifted off. And asleep in the dark, he never saw the nightmare coming.

A galvanized drainpipe isn't much, if any, protection from a massive tree. The heavy winds of the thunderstorm had washed away so much soil that it caused the tree in question to topple atop this uncompleted, uncovered drainpipe, crushing it and trapping Ron inside.

He woke to intense pain. The crushed drainpipe on his back felt like it held the weight of the Rocky Mountains. He strained to breathe. How long could he keep this up? Trying hard not to panic, Ron took as deep a breath as he could and tried to lift himself, only to collapse on his ribs, making the situation worse. His back had likely broken when the tree fell. He couldn't lift himself now, not even an inch. He wheezed an exhausted breath, fighting the pain in his back and ribs. He rested to regain whatever strength he had left.

"Focus. Stay focused, and stay positive to stay alive," he groaned to himself, trying to find his marbles in the dark. If he couldn't lift himself, maybe he could pull himself forward.

What would MacGyver do? And what can I do without MacGyver's writers to come up with something to get me out of this? Let me rest. I just need to rest. I need to think. I need to pray. Then I'll try to pull myself forward.

As he lay there, helpless and trapped, his cell phone went off: Grace, calling to tell him that she was getting some groceries and heading home and would see him soon. Crushed in the drainpipe, he could not move his arm to answer the phone or call for help. He couldn't move his legs either. In fact, he couldn't even feel his legs. The only thing he felt was trapped and powerless. How would he explain himself to her? How could he explain about Moonbeam? He hoped Moonbeam had made it out, even if he couldn't.

"Okay, now, let me see if I can pull myself forward and out of this death trap."

With a deep breath, he dragged himself forward on his palms and nearly blacked out from the pain. He couldn't move forward or backward or up. The only thing he could do was lie on his belly in the rainwater in this drainpipe. *I've got to rest and build up my strength again to try something else. I just need to rest. I just need to sleep.* Maybe if he managed to take a deep breath, he could scream at the top of his lungs, and someone would hear him. He didn't know what else to do. *I just need to rest. That's what I have to do. I need to rest, and to think positive.*

Ron believed in the power of the applied mind, in keeping a positive mental attitude. But *Oh my God. I'm stuck in this death trap. I can't think of any way out. Oh my God, I'm gonna die here. No! No! I can't think like that. If I do, I really will die. If I think like that, my will to live will die before my body does. Oh my God, I'm gonna die.* It was still raining. The wind was still howling. There was nobody out there in this weather to hear him scream, if he could scream. But he couldn't take that deep breath.

What will happen to Grace? This will devastate her. I can't give up. I just can't. Giving up, too, meant a slow, lingering death. *Oh my*

God, I'm gonna die. How could I be so stupid? Why did I put myself in this situation? And for what, a damn arrogant cat? And not only that, but how would Grace know why he was stuck in this round coffin, this metal casket? Would she know he did it all for her? *Hell no! I was too damn stupid to even leave her a note. How idiotic can I be, Lord?*

Hell, he didn't know if they would find his body. And if they did, what would people say at his funeral? "Poor, dumbass Ron died of an overdose of stupidity, and we found him in a drainage pipe." Some would wonder if he was on drugs or went nuts or something, or both, multiplied. *Actually, that theory would explain a lot with the least amount of thinking on their part.* For some, a simple explanation would be enough.

Oh God, I hope that Grace can forgive me. I did it all for her. Maybe God would tell her. That was the only hope he could muster—that Grace would know and then be able to forgive him. The hopelessness moved in and took over what little breathing space he had left, adding to the weight of the drainpipe, which was already crushing him to death.

∼

As you lie there, waiting for the arrival of death, you have time to think, to really think. Actually, you have the rest of your life to think. In this unexpectedly abbreviated, abridged life where death is your future, you wonder what and where your future will be. You have the time to judge your life as you've lived it before facing God's final judgment—time to "man up" for this last chance to be honest with yourself. Your thoughts turn toward the negatives in your life, the shortcomings by which you will be judged.

You think of everything you've left undone in this interrupted, incomplete life, now nearing its end. You think about what you've said that you shouldn't have said but did. The thoughtless, sometimes hateful words, provoked or unprovoked, that have caused so much pain. You also think about what you should have said but somehow chose not to say—words that could have eased pain, given comfort, and brought joy. Wonderful, loving things, all the I-love-yous left unsaid.

You think about the things you've done that you shouldn't have done, and the things you should have done but did not do. You think about the forgiveness you could have given but chose not to give. The forgiveness you sought but did not receive. You think about the many choices you have made in your life that might have rewritten it.

You think of your family, your friends, your coworkers, your neighbors. You wonder how they will judge your life, especially with the bizarre circumstances of your death. You hope they will remember that you were smart, funny, courageous, and an honorable man; so generous, so kind, a respected professional, and an especially devoted and loving family man. Will your unusual death redefine your entire life? Will it be the only thing they remember?

You think of the judgment of God, which lies before you, and where you will end up—what its general climate will be. As you prepare to face final judgment, what else is on your mind?

Ron sent up what he expected to be his final prayer.

"Lord, here I am, lying in this round coffin with no possible escape from this soaking-wet grave. I think I've been a good man. I strove to be wonderful to my family, my mother and father and my sister and brothers, all my life. I've been a loving husband to my beloved wife, Grace, never unfaithful. No husband has ever loved and honored his wife more than I have.

"I've been a caring father to my children. I have kept your commandments, Lord, and given my children a strong foundation in their religious beliefs and morality, and I've let them take that foundation and build their own beliefs wherever they choose to take them. I have given them a college education to provide them the best start in life I could. I am loved and respected by my friends, my coworkers, and my readers, many of whom have written to me saying how much my books have helped them in their lives.

"And this is where all my efforts, my life's work, have led me, Lord? Trapped in a wet, metal tomb with no possibility of escape? I feel that I deserve a better death, a more dignified and honorable death than this. I want to go down fighting, protecting the people I love. Yet here is where you have placed me, Lord. I'm sure you have your reasons. Perhaps my death here is to teach or test somebody in some way. I don't know. I certainly don't want to muddy the waters between us just as I am about to meet you, Lord.

"I accept the inevitable if it is your will that I die here in this place, under these circumstances. Truly, my death is likely the only way to relieve the pain in my broken body. But, Lord, the greatest, most severe pain of all lies in knowing the pain this will cause my beautiful Grace, and my children and my family—especially under these demented circumstances. My dear God, if it is your will, please find a way to ease the pain for Grace. Please create a way for her to know and understand that I ended up here out of love for her.

"She probably won't believe I could be this stupid. But as long as it is crystal clear to her why I did this, I can fully and freely accept my death. Thank you, Lord, for hearing my final prayer. Thy will be done on earth as it as it is in Heaven."

His last prayers made, Ron began to accept that he would die there. But his mind still wandered, looking for a way out. *When there is an earthquake, a building collapse, or a mine cave-in, what do the survivors think about as they lie there? Of course, they are not as alone, not as hopeless as I am. At least people know what happened to them. They know to start looking for survivors.* Nobody knew Ron was gone.

He'd always read that when people know they are dying, their whole life passes before them in the blink of an eye. Maybe in his delirium, his mind was meandering toward some goal—toward death.

Ron's mind turned once again to Grace, the true love of his life. He wanted his last living thoughts to be about her. He thought of the beautiful quirks of their relationship. For instance, whenever people asked how he and Grace met, he told them that Grace had won him in a poker game. And then there was the fact that he loved kissing Grace on her nose.

"Why do you do that, Ron?"

"Well, beautiful, it's because you're so beautiful."

"Ron, I'm as plain as a glass of water."

"Grace, you're an oasis of love in the middle of an endless desert, with palm trees and beautiful, pristine, cool water. And a waterfall, and two—count'em, two—rainbows to light the way, in Technicolor!"

He remembered telling her once, "Now, Grace dear, I do understand that you do not, or choose not to, or cannot allow yourself to see how exquisitely beautiful you are. After all, you can't even see your own forehead, or your ears, or your chin.

"You don't see yourself from the outside as I do, as everyone else does. So, you really can't see just how beautiful you truly are. Wise up! Stop looking for flaws in the diamond. Instead, realize you are an incredibly precious jewel. And if you still can't see your beauty in the mirror, just look in my eyes as I look at you, Grace. Just a sly glance from your alluring eyes and your sexy, seductive smile can turn an acorn into an oak tree. You're so hot you could burn a hole right through the sun and out the other side, and keep on going. I've told you that for years, beautiful. I hope you will come to a place where this all becomes as clear to you, my love, as it is to me and probably to every other man who sees you. I hope someday that you will see the beautiful woman that I see"

Ron recalled something he had written on a Valentine's card for Grace:

> You are the dream that made my life come true, Grace. You are indoor sunshine on a dreary, cold, and rainy day. And I am so incredibly blessed, we both are, that God put your hand in mine and both of us knew that we had found the one!

Rrring.

Grace was calling Ron's cell again. *She's worried about me. Hey, maybe they can track me down using GPS. Maybe there is hope. Maybe—*

"AHHHHHHHHHHH!"

Pain shot through his body as something chomped into his leg. Whatever it was seemed to pause at his scream, but then he felt another bite. He hadn't thought he could feel his legs and wished he still couldn't. *Oh my Lord God, something is eating me alive.* Now he screamed long and continuously, unable to move his arms or legs to fight off whatever was biting at him, tearing chunks from his legs.

As the pain overtook him, his howls of agony faded, and he lost consciousness, making way for death.

CHAPTER 3

HOME

A drenched Grace stepped through the front door and announced, "Honey, I'm home."

She expected to hear from Ron or Moonbeam, or both. She heard only the rhythmic sound of the incessant, torrential rain. She went looking for Ron so that he could help her bring in the groceries. But sick as he was, he was gone. There was no note to be found. There was no missed call on her cell phone. No trace of either Ron or Moonbeam. Did the two of them run away together? Would they end up on *Dr. Phil* or *Maury*—or, worse yet, *Jerry*?

Grace grew worried. She flashed back to her premonition from that morning that something was wrong. Maybe this was it. Ron's car was in the driveway, so he didn't drive away. Grace started to panic. She searched the house again for Ron and for Moonbeam, but all she found was Moonbeam's Thundershirt. Obviously, it had not been used to take care of Moonbeam.

"Curiouser and curiouser," she muttered, her voice shaky.

This was becoming a real mystery. She has watched enough documentaries on TV to know that in the country, the most likely explanation was alien abduction. Hell, it wasn't like it hadn't happened before!

"Maybe Ron went to the neighbors' for some reason," she suggested aloud as she retrieved the groceries from her car to bring them inside.

She called up one set of neighbors, who hadn't seen him or the cat. Now they were worried too. Grace's next-door neighbor and best friend, Sally, came over to see how she could help. They put away all the groceries, and after another thorough search of the interior and a quick once-over in the yard, Sally made some French vanilla coffee for them so that they could talk this over calmly and come up with an answer. They each had a bagel with their coffee.

"There has to be some logical explanation for this," Sally said. "Let's think this through and come up with a logical answer. We've both looked everywhere, and we couldn't find anyone. No Ron and no Moonbeam. So, Ron is not lying unconscious somewhere in the house. But you said he has a cold, or something worse. Maybe he called 911. Maybe we should try the emergency rooms or ambulance company first to eliminate those possibilities."

"Good idea, Sally. I'll call right now."

Sally continued, "But he would've called you first or while he was waiting for the ambulance. So, that's not likely. But if neither Ron nor Moonbeam is in the house, they must be somewhere outside the house."

Grace answered, "Yeah, that makes sense, Sally. But why go out in this weather? That's what's confusing me."

"The only logical reason to go outside in this weather is because you have to, but why?"

Grace considered the situation further. "Moonbeam hates the rain, the thunder, and the lightning. You know how she hides when it rains. I can't believe she would go outside. But we know she's not here in the house. Should we go outside and call and look for them? Or should we report Ron missing and let the authorities look for them? You know, since they have search dogs and such."

Sally asked, "Don't you have to wait a certain length of time before you can report a person missing?"

Grace didn't know. "Maybe not in a small town like Big Sur."

Her friend nodded. "Let's call them and get them out here to begin searching."

Grace hesitated. "We have to do something, but they might not be able to do much in this torrential rain. I mean, how can the search dogs smell?"

"Why not let the police worry about that? At least make them aware of the situation. See what they suggest we do next. We can tell them that we've already thoroughly searched the entire house and can't find Ron or the cat. And we've searched around the outside of the house. What else can we do, Grace?"

"Okay, Sally, I'll call the police."

Grace called at 1:45 p.m. The dispatcher said that with the diminished light, they couldn't promise much, but they would send a squad car right away to look around. They would ask the county to send a K-9 unit, but that would take time.

At least the proper authorities had been notified. The hardest part was the waiting.

The Big Sur police showed up a half hour later. Deputy Weber knocked on the door to get additional information from Grace. She told the deputy that her husband was sick with a cold and that if he was out in the rain, he might contract pneumonia. There was real danger there, so the need was urgent—on top of which was the fact that Ron had a serious heart condition.

Deputy Weber had a few procedural questions. Indelicate as they were, they had to be asked.

"Grace, I barely knew Ron. I've only seen him three or four times. So, let me ask you this: did Ron have some medical, emotional, or psychological condition or impairment that might have led to this situation? Was he in the military? I served in Nam, so I know how being in a war can change people. I have personal experience with PTSD. Or if he was taking any medication, perhaps he was off his meds today? That would at least give us something to go on."

Grace replied, "He was in the Marines a long time ago, but he didn't have any psychological problems or anything like that. And no, he was not off any meds. The only medications he takes are for his heart and blood pressure, nothing else, and he took both this morning."

"I understand, Grace. I'm sorry I have to ask these difficult questions. Let me call this in."

The deputy relayed the information back to headquarters and was told that a K-9 unit was already on its way to Grace's house. They were not sure how much they could do in this rain, but they would try.

Deputy Weber left to begin searching for Ron and Moonbeam. He knew that a cat was smart enough to take shelter somewhere, but he drove around and searched as best he could with his eyes.

As he expected, he only encountered more and more rain making more and more mud. Soon he got a radio call that the K-9 unit was in the vicinity. Officer Torres and his K-9 partner, German shepherd search-and-rescue dog Sigmund, were eager to begin their work. Sigmund didn't need to smell clothing from the missing person; he just searched for signs of people.

Though the rain slowed Sigmund down, it didn't stop him. He tugged as his leash, which meant he'd caught the scent of something. Any odor would be diffused and diluted, so the duo would have to investigate further.

Deputy Weber drove over to meet up with Officer Torres but stayed in his car and just watched, keeping dry. After a half hour, Torres called off the search for the night. He and Sigmund were soaked. There was little more they could do today in the rain and the dim light. They would return tomorrow and start at the spot where Sigmund had first found the scent.

Even if the rain didn't fully stop, the visibility would be exponentially better in daylight. They would also be able to get more officers into the area to help in the search.

Deputy Weber drove back to the house. He told Grace and Sally what they'd done so far. Reluctantly, he added that they had to call off the search. There was nothing else they could do tonight. Grace understood the situation and offered Deputy Weber a cup of hot coffee. He gracefully declined. His wife was worried about him too, so he had to head directly home.

Sally tried to comfort her best friend and neighbor. She reassured her that everything would work out as it should and invited Grace to dinner at her house.

"Thanks, Sally, but I need to be alone for a while. I need to think. And I want to be here if Ron comes back."

"Okay. I'll call you later if that's okay."

"Please do. Thank you, Sally. You've been so kind and thoughtful. I can't thank you enough for being here for me."

CHAPTER 4

THE SEARCH CONTINUES

Once Sally left, Grace collapsed on the sofa and cried in earnest. Perhaps this was all her fault somehow. She sobbed herself to sleep and never heard the phone ring when Sally called.

When Sally came over to check on her, she could see that Grace had been crying some of the pain out of her system. Wise, empathetic, loving Sally simply pulled a blanket over her friend and let her sleep. Sleep was what she needed most right now.

Early Wednesday morning, around ten, Grace woke to a knock on the door: Deputy Weber, along with two other officers. They told Grace that with the slightly better weather and visibility, they planned to search the entire area again.

Officer Torres had already resumed his search with his German shepherd partner. They returned to where they'd left off last night. Sigmund found the scent again and started pulling on the leash. Officer Torres tried to pull him in another direction, thinking Sigmund was confused. But Sigmund wouldn't budge. He barked to insist and then dragged Torres where the scent was leading him.

Officer Torres recognized this pattern and soon spotted the new drainpipe the county had recently started installing. Seeing the damage from the fallen tree, he realized that the drainpipe was a strong contender. Sigmund arrived at the opening and looked at

Officer Torres, barked twice, and sat to let him know that he had found the origin of the scent.

Officer Torres shined his flashlight into the drainpipe. The light didn't reach the other end; it was blocked by something large. Officer Torres had found Ron, all right.

He yelled to the figure but got no response, so he radioed an alert back to the command post and to Deputy Weber to call off the search. The missing person had been found.

"Send an ambulance, and alert the coroner."

It was now up to Deputy Weber to do the worst part of his job: informing Grace that they had found Ron in a drainpipe, and that her husband was most likely dead. He took several deep breaths and drank the last drop of his coffee.

Then he went to Grace's house and did what needed to be done.

Grace was weak kneed and stunned at the news. Her worst nightmare had come true.

Deputy Weber helped Grace to the couch. Sally put on some coffee and then held her friend tightly. Sally's presence took a lot of the pressure and responsibility off Deputy Weber, and he was glad that he only needed an ambulance for one person, not two. When he heard the sirens approach, he left Grace in Sally's capable hands to meet up with the paramedics.

The ambulance could not take Ron's body out until the tree was removed. Deputy Weber drove his squad car alongside and, using the winch attachment, looped a chain around the trunk of the tree and lifted it enough to be swung away from the drainpipe. However, the pipe was still crushed on top of Ron.

The county workers who had installed the pipe were just arriving for work and were directed to help out. They determined they would have to cut the galvanized pipe open. After some swift work, Ron's body was finally retrieved.

Everyone present saw the blood and the bites on Ron's legs. But the bites had clearly not been the cause of death. The coroner would have to figure this one out. After the paramedics confirmed that Ron was dead, they loaded him onto a gurney in the ambulance and headed to the coroner's office. The county's road crew had their work cut out for them now.

The circumstances of Ron's death would engender a great number of extended discussions over many beers. The sooner they began, the better.

～

In this small town like this, there were no reporters and no camera crews. The gossips were a lot worse than all that. They believed it their civic duty to make sure that the news was spread to the innocently curious, the "inquiring minds need to know" crowd, and the eager ghouls alike, to savor and relish. Such news made them feel alive and, of course, superior, as indeed they must in order to continue happily with their lives. In this way, the gossiping was therapeutic and beneficial: "My husband would never die in a drainpipe. I would kill him first!"

The women did their gossiping at the supermarket and the church. The speculation about what happened to Ron was creative and pointless. Many cogitated over what kinds of drugs Ron was on. Their expert opinion was that Ron had severe mental problems. After all, he was a writer; what else could you expect? The consensus was that Ron must have overdosed on some kind of "psycho" medicine or acid. Whatever the reality was, the assumption achieved its most important goal by sating their flimsy egos for the moment.

That left plenty of room for the dedicated, "expert" investigators within the gossip network to do their solemn public service by demanding details, details! They needed more details to fuel and stoke the fires of endless speculation.

The men did their gossiping at the bar. The unusual circumstance of Ron's death was by far the most compelling discussion at the local watering hole that night, even surpassing sports. The construction crew, the ambulance crew, and one police officer all made their own contributions to pander to and feed the curious and stir the pot.

Many possibilities were diligently pondered. The local experts offered their own analysis. Bets were made and polls taken. Later on, secret ballots were filled out to resolve this urgent matter democratically—video at eleven.

Somehow, all the gossipers found the strength to resist visiting Grace to offer their condolences and their comfort and perhaps bring over some food.

A lot of people were very curious about the animal bites on Ron's leg. Early Thursday morning, Doc Martin had concluded his autopsy.

He ruled out the animal bites on Ron's legs as the cause of death. No vital organs were affected. Neither was there any infection or poison involved. But the bites could have been a contributing factor in his death. The true cause was a heart attack brought on by stress: likely the stress of Ron's essentially being buried and then eaten alive, unable to defend himself.

Furthermore, after investigating animal hairs near the wound, Doc Martin determined that the animal bites were from a bobcat or possibly a young mountain lion. How and why Ron came to be in that position inside a drainage pipe was for someone else to determine.

CHAPTER 5

A KNOCK AT THE DOOR

Sally did all she could for her dear best friend and neighbor, sparing Grace what pain she could. She made the phone calls to Ryder, Melody, and everyone else who needed to know. She made the funeral arrangements, and the funeral parlor placed an obituary in the newspaper. Everything was done properly, and everything was in place and underway.

Grace thanked her profusely. Never one to do things halfway, Sally even made dinner for her friend and helped her to bed. Grace gracefully refused her offer to stay over, so Sally headed home and tried to sleep as well.

Grace needed the quiet time alone to adjust to the sudden vacuum in her life. She still didn't know why Ron and Moonbeam had gone out in the rain. Maybe the answers would come to her in a dream. Maybe Ron would come to her in a dream.

How could this happen to us? she wondered, bewildered. *We're such kind, loving people. We had such a wonderful future planned. We finally had time to enjoy each other fully, just the two of us. Now, all of a sudden, all those plans and all those dreams are gone forever. And my children no longer have a father to love them and help guide them. Who will walk Melody down the aisle and give her away at her wedding?*

She couldn't believe that she had to bury her husband, their love, their dreams, and her own future. And she didn't know why. *Why, Ron, why did you go out in the rain when you were so sick? You must have had a reason. What was it?*

Her tears were overtaken, mercifully, by sleep.

∼

Thursday morning, after Grace had heard the coroner's conclusions, Sally came over to take care of her. She noted that the food she had left outside for Moonbeam was gone, but she didn't know whether a wild animal had eaten it. She elected not to mention anything to Grace.

She made a pot of Irish cream coffee while she prepared breakfast. As the two ladies were finishing up their coffee, they heard a knock at the door. Maybe some of Grace's friends were finally coming over to comfort her? Grace and Sally both went to answer the door. On the porch stood an unfamiliar woman.

"Good morning, Mrs. Butler. You don't know me, as there has been no occasion for us to meet. First of all, let me offer my condolences for the loss of your husband, Ron. But that is not the reason why I came to see you. I'm here for a very special reason. This likely sounds strange, even intrusive, especially at this tragic time, but I am a psychic medium. And I have a very important message for you from your late husband."

Startled and astonished, yet ever courteous, Grace said, "Won't you please come in? This is my neighbor and dear friend Sally." They gathered in the kitchen, and Grace poured her guest some coffee. "Here, have a cup of coffee, and we'll talk. And you needn't be so formal. Please, call me Grace."

The medium grasped the mug in both hands as they settled at the kitchen table. She met Grace's eyes firmly.

"Okay, Grace. Ron wants me to explain why he was out in really bad weather, stuck inside a drainpipe with a severe cold and a heart condition. You see, Grace, you wanted him to stay home and take care of himself. You also told Ron to make sure to get that Thundershirt on Moonbeam because otherwise she goes deep into hiding when the weather gets bad to protect herself. Knowing how important she is to you, Ron would have done anything, regardless of risk or cost, to take care of Moonbeam. And that is exactly what he did; he took care of Moonbeam.

"After you left for the doctor's office, Ron went looking for Moonbeam to put the Thundershirt on her. He looked everywhere in the house, twice. Then he stopped, sat down, and thought about where she might go. He reasoned that if he had looked in every place where Moonbeam could hide in the house, she must be somewhere he had not looked yet; she must be outside. So, sick as he was, he went out into the 'aquatic unknown,' as he called it, to search the only logical place where Moonbeam might have gone: the woods.

"Nutty as that sounds, that is what Ron was thinking. He felt that Moonbeam had disappeared on his watch. To lose the cat that you love so much, Grace, was something he could not allow to happen. He was determined to do whatever it took to save her. He went looking all around, calling, 'Moonbeam, Moonbeam, where are you? Come to Daddy, Moonbeam.' His search led him to the one place a hysterical cat could find shelter from the storm: the drainpipe. And lo and behold, he heard something meowing inside!

"So, Grace, with so much love in his heart for you, he climbed into the drainpipe to look for Moonbeam. He thought he had finally found her and could bring her home safely, and you would never have known that she was out at all, and you wouldn't be mad at him.

"And if the rain and the wind and the soil erosion hadn't conspired to cause the tree to fall on the drainpipe, he would've been able to crawl out of the other end and get home safely, and all would be well. But unfortunately, the tree did fall on the drainpipe, crushing his back and ribs and leaving him powerless to help himself, or Moonbeam.

"But there is more that I have to tell you, something even Ron didn't know about. A mother bobcat had brought her young kittens to safety from the rain inside the drainpipe. These were the meows he heard. When the bobcat returned to check on her kittens, she thought they were being attacked by a large predator. She did what any mother would do to protect her young: she attacked the predator and bit his legs. Everything happening together—the crushed ribs, the broken back, and all the stress and the biting pain—caused Ron to have a heart attack, which caused his death.

"That's what he wanted you to know, Grace. So, when everyone wonders if he was a mental case or on drugs or something, at least you'll know why he was in the drainpipe. And perhaps you can find some solace and healing in knowing that.

"I've now done what Ron has asked me to do. He is more at peace now, and hopefully you are too, Grace."

Grace and Sally sat in dumbfounded silence, trying to process this stranger's words.

The psychic medium continued, "I never met Ron in the conventional, earthly sense, but I really like him. I especially love the love he has for you. And I happen to be in a position to know that love, true love, is for all eternity.

"You see, Grace, love doesn't end. The love between you and Ron has become immortal, eternal, and even more loving. In other words, you and Ron are destined to be together again. That is a fact. Love doesn't end; it transcends life. It rises above life as you know it."

Grace and Sally were quite astonished by this revelation.

"And now I have to go. I have other work to do."

"Wait! I don't even know your name," Grace pleaded.

"It's probably best that you don't know my name for now, although we may meet again. Whatever God has planned, I have other work to do. Other people need me. But be reassured that if you truly need me, I will know, and I will come to you. I go where there is a need—where God sends me.

"I hope I have been helpful to you, Grace, and to you, Sally, as well. Go with God. And go with Ron's everlasting love."

With that being said, with that being done, she left.

Grace and Sally stared at each other for a good minute, stunned, dazed, and amazed. Then they hugged and cried in each other's arms. Grace cried for Ron, and for Moonbeam, wherever that silly beast was. Sally cried for her late husband, Owen, whom she had lost eight years earlier. Together they now found comfort in knowing the transcendence of love, and each found some small peace from their pain.

CHAPTER 6

OBLIGATIONS AND RESPONSIBILITIES

That beautiful moment ended with a phone call from the funeral parlor. Sally rose to speak with them, but Grace felt well enough to take care of things for herself now. The funeral parlor wanted to go over schedules and timetables for Ron's viewing on Friday and the funeral on Saturday.

Grace planned for four people to speak at the funeral. Their priest, Father Jerry Williams, would speak first, then Ryder and Melody would speak together, and Grace would close. The funeral parlor said they had made all the preparations and printed up the necessary documents. The viewing would occur Friday from 4 to 9 p.m. The funeral would be Saturday at 11 a.m.

All the phone calls to friends and family were made. Ryder and Melody would be arriving that afternoon, in about an hour or so. Ryder's friend Billy planned to pick both of them up from the airport and drive them to Grace's house. Meanwhile, Grace and Sally picked out the clothes Ron would be buried in and what Grace would wear for the viewing and the funeral.

There was nothing left to do but prepare mentally and emotionally for this unavoidable responsibility.

Ryder and Melody got out of the car and let themselves in. As Billy carried the twins' luggage to the house, Sally hugged and kissed them. Her eyes spoke volumes about the anguish they all shared. Ryder and Melody embraced their mother, who was frail and wet after many hours of shedding tears that never dried. No words were spoken, because there were no words. The only communication was from heart to heart to heart.

Sally hugged Billy in commiseration; it was painful to watch what their loved ones were going through. Emotional and uncomfortable, Billy felt like he shouldn't intrude on such a private family moment.

Sally sensed his unease and handed over Ron's clothes to take to the funeral parlor, telling Billy that he could express his condolences to Grace at the viewing tomorrow. He was grateful to be given something useful to do and left the family to their intimate pain. Sally made coffee, discreetly leaving the room so the family could talk.

After a long, solemn, silent hug of shock and agony between Grace and the kids, they sat to talk.

"Mom, Sally called us to let us know what happened to Dad. She said you were so devastated that you couldn't talk much, and she wanted to save you some of the torment of having to tell us," Melody said quietly.

After a deep breath, Grace said, "Thank God for Sally. She has been such an incredibly loving friend. I'm not sure I would be standing here without her strength in guiding me, carrying me, and pushing and pulling me along. I'm sure you've heard a lot of rumors and speculation about what happened to your dad."

The twins nodded hesitantly.

"Let me tell you the truth as I know it. You both know how Moonbeam is scared to death of thunder and lightning. Well, I had to go to the doctor's office on Tuesday, and it was a rainy, windy day. Your father was too sick to accompany me. Anyway, she must have really freaked out when I wasn't there to comfort her, because when Dad went looking for her to put on her Thundershirt and calm her down, he couldn't find her anywhere. He started to panic.

"Dad finally reasoned that a hysterical cat might do something crazy and run out of the house and into the rain. So, he went looking for her in the thunderstorm. He heard a meowing sound from a drainpipe and thought it was Moonbeam. Then he crawled inside to rescue her.

"Your dad crawled further and further into the drainpipe, thinking he was getting closer and closer to Moonbeam. But I've learned that the meowing actually came from some bobcat kittens. While he was deep in the drainpipe, a large tree fell on top and crushed it, trapping your father inside. He was paralyzed, unable to move. His back was broken, and his ribs were broken. And as he lay there, he was attacked and bitten on the legs by the mama bobcat, who thought she was protecting her kittens from a large predator.

"Your dad's powerlessness, the stress, and the pain gave him a heart attack. This was the cause of death. A K-9 unit eventually found him, and he was removed from the drainpipe." She choked back a sob. "He went after Moonbeam to protect and save her because he knew how much I loved her. He did it for me because he loved me so much."

Grace toppled into a bottomless well of tears. Her children tried to console her, but Grace was inconsolable. Melody could only hold her. Ryder sat with his head in his hands. His sister settled her free hand on his shoulder to provide some warmth, if not comfort. Moonbeam's continued absence went unaddressed. Now was not the time.

Sally brought in a tray with a coffee pot, cups, and some sandwiches and cookies. Setting it on the coffee table in front of them, she went back to the kitchen. She was drinking her coffee at the kitchen table when Melody came in to speak with her about twenty minutes later.

Melody put her coffee cup on the table next to Sally's. They were both so eloquent in their silence, with little to say but much to endure. Sally didn't want to speak first, but Melody struggled for words. Sally saved her by telling her that she was planning a family get-together at her house both tonight and Saturday night. She asked whether Melody and Ryder could help her with the preparations, but she didn't really need their help. She just wanted to shift their focus from something negative to something more positive and constructive for the family.

Ryder eventually joined them in the kitchen, reporting that Grace had fallen asleep on the couch. Sally suggested that Melody and Ryder find some photos of Ron to display for any friends and family who came by. She wanted them to select images that would bring up fond memories: birthday, vacation, and Christmas photos and such. Sally also suggested that they exhibit Ron's books and writing awards. She wanted everyone to know what an incredible man their dad was—not merely a man who died stuck in a drainpipe, but a successful writer and a devoted husband and father who would give anything for the people he loved.

Dinner would be at Sally's house tonight at seven. Now they had a plan.

∼

That night, Grace, Melody, and Ryder arrived at Sally's house precisely on time. Somber faced under the weight of their individual and collective loss, none of them said much amid the soft, soothing background music of Chopin's The Nocturnes, a famous piece of classical music. The solemn solo piano matched what everyone was feeling.

Although they were all in Sally's kitchen, they were also somewhere else—wherever their grief took them to. Sally had wanted to provide this solace to them, to give them a safe, familiar place where they could grieve in peace without being surrounded by reminders of what they had lost.

Sally asked Ryder and Melody to help her set the table. She would be the mommy for all of them tonight, including Grace.

With the table set and everyone seated around it, she looked at each of them in turn.

"Okay, everybody, this is where we all hold hands and say grace and give thanks. I'll start: Lord God, thank you so much for lifting us up and carrying each of us individually, and all of us together, through these oh-so-difficult times. When love is ripped out of our hearts and our lives so suddenly, we don't have time to prepare ourselves. We are filled with sudden, unexpected, monumental grief and many, many responsibilities.

"Thank you so much, Lord, for creating a path for us and keeping us moving forward. And thank you so much for carrying us down that path during those times when we couldn't move forward or even stand. May the food before us feed and sustain our bodies as your love sustains our spirits. Thank you so much, Lord. Amen."

Everyone stared emptily at each other for a moment. Sally started eating, signaling everyone else to follow suit. No one knew what to do or say. Finally, Grace "manufactured" conversation to fill the void, to get from one minute to the next. She asked the twins how things were going at their schools.

Picking up on their mother's need to get them through the evening and encouraged that she seemed more lucid now, Ryder and Melody shared stories about their college activities and courses of study. The somewhat longwinded, inane conversation filled the space and served the purpose of helping time move along. Eventually, the family ran out of things to say.

During dinner, Sally started smiling, though she tried to conceal it. Grace asked her what she was laughing about.

Sally said, "I was remembering the time when you guys had everyone over that Fourth of July, and Ron was grilling hot dogs and hamburgers. A hot dog got away and somehow got to a place where Ron couldn't reach it on a very hot grill. It fell inside it or something.

"Ron let all the other food almost burn trying to get that hot dog. He refused to accept that a hot dog could outsmart him. That insolent little 'tube steak' had to be punished and taught a lesson as a warning to all other hot dogs. Ron would not tolerate a rebellion on his grill, no matter what."

Everyone chuckled, remembering the incident. It was so Ron to never give up. For the next two hours, they all chimed in with their own funny Ron stories. Sally had achieved her goal. They were mentally and emotionally present, and everyone was laughing. The spell was broken, if only for a short time. They had made it through this Thursday night.

When it was time to get some sleep and get ready for tomorrow, they all hugged and kissed and thanked Sally.

Between the family, Sally, and the funeral home, everything was planned and arranged and underway. Everyone was so exhausted from the stress, the grief, and the overflow of emotion that they were all in bed and asleep in about ten minutes, each to their own dreams and wherever sleep might take them.

CHAPTER 7

THE WAKE

Early Friday morning, Grace made blueberry pancakes in honor of the last meal Ron had prepared for her. It made her feel more connected to her late husband.

Grace yelled to her family, "Breakfast is ready. Get it while it's hot"—just as Ron had yelled to her on that fateful morning.

"Be right there," Ryder and Melody called simultaneously. Just as Grace had said to Ron.

Rather than sensing this reprise as a tragic "history repeating itself" moment, Grace found it comforting in a "Life goes on" kind of way. A happy sad, not a sad sad.

Sally arrived at the breakfast table before Melody and Ryder. She had gone to the market for fresh fruit in case anybody wanted a healthier alternative to pancakes.

To everyone's amusement, both Melody and Ryder wore two different NC State Wolfpack sweatshirts to honor their dad. The foursome was surprised and delighted to find themselves laughing once again—laughing partly because the happenstance was unexpected and partly because the twins rarely agreed on anything. A great deal of pain quietly slipped away, hidden inside the laughter. And that helped a lot, even if they didn't realize it at the moment.

After breakfast, the phone rang. The local TV station had seen the obituary in the paper. Well aware of the gossip and speculation surrounding Ron's death, they inquired about the unusual circumstances. Some of their viewers wanted to know the more titillating details.

Grace responded with a terse "No comment!" and hung up in as ladylike a manner as she could muster.

It was clear by now that none of Grace's other "friends" would be coming over to see her and comfort her. Perhaps they would see her at the wake or the funeral.

∼

Later that afternoon, Sally and the family dressed in their wake clothes and headed to the funeral home to do their unavoidable duty. Sally went in first to speak to the funeral director. He came out and greeted everyone, extending his condolences. He then reported that everything was ready and asked if they would like private time with Ron before the others arrived. They all stared at each other and with their silent eyes agreed to go into the viewing room as a family.

They entered slowly, at first focusing on the flowers and the photos and avoiding the casket. Then Sally took Grace's hand, and they approached the coffin together. Sally tugged slightly at Grace as she walked, guiding her and giving her the energy and strength to do what needed to be done.

When they reached Ron's casket, Sally released her friend's hand and went back to sit with Ryder and Melody. Sally's goal was not to see Ron but to give Grace the strength to do so. They all gave Ron's widow a quiet moment to spend with her late husband.

Grace gazed lovingly at her husband for a long while. Sally, Melody, and Ryder saw her mouth moving but could not hear her words. Witnessing her last, private conversation with the love of her life brought the pain to the surface in all its glory—a stabbing, burning pain. And imagining the anguish his mother felt pushed

Ryder over the edge. Everything came out of him at once. Under the weight of the pain and anger, he fell to his knees. He was powerless to defeat his mother's suffering, so he beat himself up inside instead.

Melody leaned over to try and comfort him, but Sally stopped her and embraced her.

"Better to let him get some of this out of his system now," Sally whispered. "It has been building up for days. I know you understand that having no chance to say goodbye hurt him quite severely. Remember how close they were. But I imagine what hurts him most of all is that he can't do anything about it. That fact is agonizing to all of us."

When his sobs had faded, Sally murmured, "We can check on him now."

The twins shared a long, tight hug.

Once Grace finally joined the other three in the row of chairs, Melody softly asked what she had said to Ron.

Grace replied, "At first, I just looked at him, trying to send all the love I hold for him to his spirit. Then I told him how incredibly loving and brave he was to go out in the thunderstorm to rescue Moonbeam and how proud I am of him. I told him that I know he sacrificed everything for me, for our love.

"I wondered how I could ever repay such a great act of love. What can I do to honor and carry on all that great love he showed me? Then it came to me. I can do so by writing books, by continuing and completing some of Ron's story ideas. I don't know if it will help his legions of fans, but I do know that it will help me."

The others enveloped her in an incredible group hug that seemed to last for hours. Then Melody took Ryder's hand, and they walked together to the casket. Their communication with their father was internal and silent. Still holding hands, they returned to Grace and Sally for another group hug. A moment later, the first influx of family and friends came into the viewing room.

The immediate family's responsibilities shifted.

They hugged each and every family member and friend who came by. The first of the family to arrive were Ron's twin brothers and his sister and their spouses. The twins, Jerry and Frank, were devastated when they first heard, but Molly was downright traumatized. Her husband had needed to call 911, and after two hours in the ER, Molly awoke in more tears. She and the twins had been planning a surprise fortieth wedding anniversary event for Ron and Grace. They had arranged to fly the couple to Hawaii, which Ron and Grace long dreamed of visiting, making the news all the more crushing.

A Niagara Falls of tears took over the proceedings. No one could speak. But the love they shared spoke volumes and was heard and understood by all present, including Melody and Ryder, who stood slightly apart from their mother. They were way too emotional to remain huddled in a group when they had so many responsibilities to take care of.

Ron's siblings then commiserated with their nephew and niece, and, once again, words were hopelessly inadequate. They did not say half as much as the hugs and tears. Molly and the twins moved on to thank Sally for holding everything together under such terrible circumstances.

More people trickled in for Ron's wake. Finally, their priest, Father Jerry, arrived with a few of Ron's old friends from a previous job. Ron's literary agent, Bobby Simon, and longtime publisher, Paul Wallace, appeared together. Some of Grace's friends and former coworkers from the school came by to offer their condolences and their comfort. Ryder and Melody's friends arrived with their respective parents. Later, a couple of Ron and Grace's neighbors stopped by.

Everything seemed to take forever and a half. A few of Melody and Ryder's mutual friends wanted to give them a break, so they slipped outside for a while, sitting in the courtyard on some benches. The friends didn't speak about Ron at all. They wanted to reduce the pressure, not add to it. Instead, they discussed the concerts they had attended and how great they were and then asked the twins about college life.

They were gone for about fifteen minutes. Once back inside, Ryder and Melody suggested to Sally that she and Mom take a break as well. Sally thought that was a great idea.

Ryder and Melody took the lead in greeting and thanking each attendee for coming to their father's wake while Sally discreetly dragged her friend off to get some coffee. Grace was reluctant but soon realized she needed the respite.

Few seemed to notice her absence. The crowd was busy paying their respects to Ron and checking their watches. After all, nobody wants to be in a funeral parlor. They were there because they had to be. Non-family members spoke among themselves until each of them in turn felt that the time was right to leave for the evening.

The night was dark and starless. Ever wise, ever thoughtful, Sally led Grace to the coffee shop just down the street, away from the bustle of the parlor and the eerie quiet of the attached courtyard.

"Grace, you're doing fantastic under these unbelievable circumstances. You've done everything perfectly for Ron, for yourself, and for your family and friends. But all this is so overwhelming. Believe me, I know. You need to pace yourself."

Sally continued, "The funeral is tomorrow morning. There will be even more stress and pressure on you at the cemetery. So, take some time to take care of you. Drink some tea; eat something. We'll go back in about fifteen minutes. The whole process is moving along just as planned, but you'll need your strength. We'll go back, and you'll feel better and better able to handle all this. Okay? You just have to take a little time to take care of yourself, Grace."

When Grace and Sally got back, they went right over to check on Melody and Ryder. Then they approached Molly and the older twins.

Molly said, "This might sound strange, but I think my brother would approve of the way things worked out for the wake and for the funeral tomorrow."

The twins agreed. "It certainly helps that the funeral is on a Saturday," Frank added. "We spoke with most of the people attending today, and they said they would be there. Once again, thank you, Sally, for all you've done for Grace and the kids. You're more than a close friend. You're family, just as much as we are. In fact, you are our guardian angel, heaven sent to carry all of us through this ordeal. Thank you for being so strong, wise, and so very loving."

Time for another heartfelt group hug. Other folks in the room teared up, leading to an outbreak of group hugs around the room. Then the remaining visitors seemed to simultaneously realize that it was time to go home for the night. They all had an early Saturday morning to prepare for.

This night's ordeal was almost over. Soon, only Sally, Grace, Ryder, and Melody remained. They all took a breather, and after a final look at Ron, they were ready to leave.

Sally announced, "Let's go get a steak dinner. It was Ron's favorite. I'm buying. Dennison's should still be open."

CHAPTER 8

AFTER THE WAKE

The group felt slightly refreshed when they arrived at Dennison's. With the pressure of the wake over with, they could relax a little.

"What did Ron usually order?" Sally asked Grace.

"He always ordered a nine-ounce sirloin steak, medium rare."

Melody chimed in, "And he would get a Caesar salad and a loaded baked potato."

"He always asked for a root beer, which Dad knew they never had," Ryder added. "He just liked to bust their chops. He would get a Diet Coke instead."

They all responded with a variation on "Yeah, sounds like Ron, all right."

"That's what I'll have, a dinner for Ron," Sally announced.

Grace smiled. "I'll have that too."

"Let's all have that," said Melody, ignoring the fact that Ron's usual order would probably have fed any two of them.

Once they'd given their identical orders to the bemused waiter, Grace said, "Sally, you are so wise. Frank was right: you take such good care of us."

This statement was followed by—guess what—another long group hug at Sally's chair. For a few people from the wake who were also having a late dinner at Dennison's, seeing the group hug at the Butlers' table inspired them to treasure their loved ones all the more. They expressed their love with a teary-eyed communal hug at their own table, making Grace even more appreciative of what she still had.

Talk strayed far from the topic of the wake until they'd received their food. This reminder of Ron turned to talk of his siblings.

Sally commented, "It was really good to see Molly and the twins. I haven't seen them since forever. But I think that Molly's hearing is even worse than the last time I saw them."

Ryder responded, "Yeah, Uncle Jerry and Uncle Frank told me that without her hearing aids, the only thing loud enough for her to hear now are TV commercials."

Nobody laughed as they munched on their steaks. It was just too true to be funny.

"Too bad Ron couldn't grill a steak nearly as well as they make here at Dennison's," Sally quipped.

Recalling the steak in question, Ryder quickly replied, "You're so right. My friends and I played hockey with that overcooked puck. I scored three goals—a hat trick."

A few chuckles followed.

Melody put in her two cents: "The best thing about dad's grilling was that we all survived and went on to lead more or less normal lives. Thanks, Dad."

Now everyone broke up in full laughter. Nobody disagreed with Melody's comment.

Soon it was time to go home and get ready for tomorrow.

Standing on the porch as Ryder unlocked the front door, Grace said, "I'll make some coffee, tea, or hot chocolate. What does everybody want?"

"I'm wiped out. I just want to go to bed," Ryder said, opening the door and turning to face them from the threshold.

Melody agreed. "Big day tomorrow. I'm ready to go to sleep right now."

"Good night, everybody. Thanks again, Aunt Sally," Ryder said.

With a small smile, Grace bid her children good night.

"Well, Sally, it's just you and me."

"I'm even sleepier than the kids," Sally protested. "I'm heading for bed."

"Of course. You've earned it. Just wave from the kitchen window when you get there, okay?"

"Okay, Grace."

Once Sally had waved, Grace gave herself permission to sleep as well.

Meanwhile, instead of going right to bed, Melody and Ryder had a chat in Ryder's room.

"How do you think Mom is doing, Rye Bread? Do you think her grief has made her clinically depressed?"

"You're the one with the medical background. What do you think?"

"I think she's handling everything really well under the circumstances—thanks in large part to Sally. I mean, she's having a normal response to the loss of her husband, just like we are to our father's death. I don't think there's a medical or psychological crisis here. But I'll ask Father Jerry to speak to Mom when he thinks the timing is right. Maybe he can recommend a good therapist who has a lot of experience with grief counseling."

"Good idea, Mel. Let's speak to him together after the funeral, okay?"

"That sounds right. Good. We have a plan. I'll see you in the morning, Rye Bread."

"Good night, Mallomars. You get some sleep."

~

Everybody slept late the day of Ron's funeral and were still in deep slumber when Sally came over and let herself in. She gently knocked on their bedroom doors.

"It's Sally. Time to wake up. I'm making breakfast now. We all have a lot to do today, so let's get started."

Sally put the coffee on downstairs and got the griddle ready, then set the table.

One by one, they others staggered into the kitchen. One by one, they all hugged and kissed Sally, thanking her yet again for her thoughtfulness.

"Do we win a prize when we give you the millionth thank-you, Sally?" Grace asked.

Sally responded, "Congratulations, Grace, the prize is a hot breakfast! Eat it while it's hot. We have to get dressed and head for the church in an hour and a half. We *cannot* be late."

They finished breakfast swiftly, leaving the plates and cookware in the sink for later. The first to finish, Sally hurried back to her house to get dressed and ready to go. Everybody else fell quiet as they retired to their rooms to dress and consider what they would say at the funeral.

The rain had finally slowed down. According to the weatherman, they might actually have sunshine tomorrow. But, appropriately, not today.

An hour later, Sally returned to Grace's house to make sure everybody was on schedule.

"It's Sally," she shouted upstairs. "Is everyone ready or almost ready?"

Grace said, "Five more minutes, and I'll be down."

Melody responded, "I'm just finishing my hair, Sally."

"Just fixing my tie. I'll be there in a minute," Ryder added.

Fifteen minutes later, they were all downstairs, asking each other if they looked okay.

Well, we're pretty much on schedule. That is really quite amazing! Sally thought.

Ryder went out to start the car as Melody put the final touches on her mother's hair. By 10 a.m., they were all ready to go.

CHAPTER 9

THE FUNERAL

The church was a relatively short, fifteen-minute drive away, so they arrived forty-five minutes before the crowd was scheduled to show. Father Jerry Williams, who had been a close friend of Ron's, greeted them warmly.

The priest reassured them that everything was ready at the church and at the cemetery. He went over the schedule of events, including the order in which they would speak. It had been previously agreed that Molly and the twins would not be speaking; Molly was too fragile, and the twins wanted to give the younger generation of twins plenty of time to say what needed to be said.

Father Jerry suggested they take time to settle in and say their last farewells to Ron. One by one, they approached the casket. One by one, they sat in the first pew to ready themselves for the service, holding hands for support.

As expected, Ron's siblings arrived first. There was once again more hugging than speaking, everyone so overwhelmed with emotion that words were useless. But Molly had something important to add.

"Grace, after the cemetery, we planned to go to Angelo's restaurant. It's a quiet place where we can have some good food along with the privacy we all need. Everything is arranged, and we've already paid for it. We will have nothing to worry about. We can just be together and start to put Ron's funeral behind us and make peace with what our lives will become. I just wanted you to not have that worry on your mind."

Grace expressed her immense gratitude.

"It's nothing. We're family. All of us take care of all of us."

With that said, they took their seats. More people came in and found seats. By 10:45, it seemed everyone had arrived.

Father Jerry made his way to the pulpit and, at 11 a.m. sharp, began the service.

"Thank you, everyone, for coming to this service. We are all here to honor and pay our final respects to Ronald James Butler as we say our farewells. Believe me, I know how difficult it has been. Many of us had planned to gather next month for a much happier occasion, the wedding of two of our congregants. Instead, we are gathered here in sadness for the funeral of a man whom we dearly loved and admired.

"Ron was and still is my best friend. Ours was a friendship I have greatly treasured, taken great pride in, and nurtured over a lifetime. In fact, I had the high honor of performing the wedding ceremony for Ron and Grace almost forty years ago. I was so very happy for my best friend and his beautiful bride, Grace. They had the kind of relationship that makes even cynics believe in love again. I knew that my best friend had found his soulmate.

"When Ron and Grace were together, they made their own sunshine—bright, loving, and healing. Their families and friends basked in the warm glow of their love every chance they got. Aristotle wrote, 'Love consists of one soul inhabiting two bodies.' He was obviously talking about Grace and Ron. When you saw how perfect they were together, a wide, unexpected smile came over you. Everyone wanted what they had—and still have! But no one felt jealous of them. They just felt happy. Uplifted. Optimistic. That was the effect of their love.

"The circumstances of Ron's death are filled with mystery, confusion, and uncertainty. However, the impact of Ron's death is clear and illuminating. We are all different people to the different people in our lives. We have all had different experiences with Ron, different memories, different funny stories.

"Ron the fighter always had the courage to say to the city council what so many of us thought but were not in a position to articulate. Ron the leader would keep our discussions civil and orderly so all of us could have our say, eventually arrive at a consensus, and be able to move forward. He made sure we respected each other so we could all remain friends. Ron the comedian was the funniest guy any of us knew. I was blessed to know all of those Rons, though I'm sure there were others.

"But the common thread, what shows through, is that Ron was a fiercely dedicated family man who would go above and beyond above and beyond. We were lucky to know him—far and away the greatest friend a person could have."

Father Jerry continued, "Ron Butler and I were best friends from a very early age. We grew up in the same neighborhood. We played together after school and on the weekends. We did all the things, both good and bad, that best friends do. Of course, that didn't stop Ron from pulling pranks on me and busting my chops. But he also scared off the tough guys who tried to bully me. They were afraid of Ron. He put the 'Ron' in 'Ironman.'

"Ron and I joined the Marines together, and we served together. After we were both honorably discharged, I went to the seminary, and Ron went to college. He studied hard and became a writer. He worked for a newspaper back in the days when there were still newspapers. I watched my best friend become a successful, published, award-winning author. Of course, that still didn't stop him from pulling the occasional prank on me—most recently, three years ago.

"I'm too much of a gentleman and far too embarrassed to tell you what that prank was, even though Ron would probably want me to so that he could enjoy that laugh all over again. I told him that if he pulled one more prank on me, just one, I would use all of my contacts, everywhere, in heaven, among the saints, on earth—and I know a lot of people—and even in hell to give him the punishment he so richly deserved. Yeah, that's right. Some important people down there owe me a few favors. We both had a good laugh about that one.

"Now I'm leading a funeral service for my best friend, and I am so emotionally overwrought that I don't know what to do or say next. Just like everyone else, I never got a chance to say goodbye. I never got a chance to tell him how much I loved him. Or how much I admired and respected him. And how he did so much to encourage, help, and guide me—and sometimes carry me or yell at me or grab me by the shirt and shake me good when he thought I needed it. That is what best friends do for each other.

"I don't know if many of you know that Ron is why I became a Catholic priest. Like best friends do, we would talk for hours and hours, about anything and everything. I was going back and forth, wondering if I should enter the seminary or not. There is a great deal to consider in taking such an important step and much that you have to leave behind you.

"What made me finally end my waffling was a critically important conversation with my best friend. Ron could see the wheels turning in my head. He said, 'Jerry, what are you waiting for? Do I have to push you off the diving board and into the pool? Do I have to wrap your arms and legs up in wet sheets, drop you off at the door of the seminary, and honk the horn as I drive away? What the hell are you waiting for? Go and fulfill your destiny; serve God and serve your fellow man. You have a great chance of making it to heaven's Hall of Fame. So, go, and go today, right now!'

"Needless to say, Ron drove me to the seminary, and we went inside together. Then, Ron left me in their hands. And thus began my service to God and man. And it brings me here before you today for this somber tribute to my beloved friend. I may not be the best person to preside over these services because I am so emotionally invested. I couldn't let a stranger send him off, but I tell you, if I wasn't here at the pulpit, I would be crying my eyes out in a pew.

"I don't want to linger too long on my own loss. Instead, I want to bring up Ron and Grace's children, Melody and Ryder, to speak with you. Will you please come up here now?"

Ryder and Melody held hands once again as they ascended to the pulpit and the microphone. They needed each other's support to get through this, so they had decided to speak together. At first, they merely looked at each other, neither able to begin. Finally, Melody spoke.

"Thank you, Father Jerry, and thank all of you for coming out today to honor our father, Ron Butler."

Encouraged by her strength, Ryder interjected, "This is so much more difficult than I imagined. What can we say to do justice to our father's life? How do we summarize who he was and tell you what a wonderful and loving father and husband he was?"

Melody said, "Even if my brother and I had three wishes each, we couldn't have wished for a more patient, a more loving, a more understanding or generous father. We are proud to carry his name. And we're so very proud to be the products of such a blessed, loving marriage."

Ryder added, "God has been generous with our family. Growing up, my sister and I saw every day what a marriage should look like. Our parent's marriage and our upbringing are the models we intend to follow to find wonderful, loving companions for ourselves."

Melody continued, "Our father was and still is the firm foundation for our lives. He made all of us feel secure and confident in ourselves. He told us that anything our minds could conceive, we could achieve—anything! That is incredibly reassuring to a kid and has been the basis for so many of my accomplishments, and for Ryder's. So, you can imagine how crushing his loss is for us."

Ryder said, "We couldn't bring ourselves to think of and share all the fun things we did as a family—all the vacations, the fun, goofy times we spent together, and the embarrassing photos that commemorated those times. We are all in mourning right now. I know those memories will eventually come back to us and make us smile." Here he had to pause and swallow back the tears. "But the pain has strangled the words to convey them. We're just doing what we can to honor our father and mother. And speaking about what a wonderful, giving man our father was is the most I can manage."

Ryder turned his head away from the audience to wipe away the flood of tears. But he had gotten through it.

Melody closed by saying, "As my brother said, this is incredibly difficult. We've all lost so very, very much. We are still in shock. We have to get back to our mother. We need her right now."

With that, they both returned to their seats and gripped Grace's hands tightly. Father Jerry came back to the pulpit.

"Thank you, Melody and Ryder."

CHAPTER 10

GRACE'S EULOGY FOR RON

Father Jerry continued, "The last person to speak today will be Ron's loving wife, Grace. One of their first dates was at a dinner in my home. Ron wanted me to meet her so I could see in person just how beautiful, how wonderful and loving she is. She is as incredible as he said, and more so. I now ask that my dear friend Grace Butler come up here and speak to us."

In the first pew, Sally gave Grace a warm hug of strength, support, and encouragement. Grace somehow made it up to the pulpit on wobbly legs.

"Thank you so much, Father . . . Williams. I'm so sorry, Father; I almost called you Jerry. I thank you all so very much for being here. Thank you for being part of this outpouring of love as we celebrate the life of my husband, the love of my life, Ronald James Butler.

"It is unbearably difficult to be here, speaking with you at my husband's funeral. It's hard to stand here at all on such shaky legs. None of us had a chance to say goodbye to Ron. I had no way to know that our kiss on Tuesday morning was the last kiss, forever and ever. The night before, I had a nightmare that would send chills down even Stephen King's spine. And Stephen King puts the 'boo' in books! But my nightmare was no fiction. What compels me to remain standing is the duty to give testament to the incredible love Ron and I shared.

That great love gives me the strength, somehow, to speak at all.

"Ron wrote in one of his books, 'Love, like life, is so brief, so fleeting, so fragile, so vulnerable.' Who knows that better than me? I've lived for sixty-four years. I've been married to Ron for thirty-nine of them. But I've not lived nearly long enough or learned nearly enough to begin to contemplate such an incalculable loss—the loss of everything there is in my life, it seems. I've been calling it 'the Great Eclipse' in my mind. When the light of Ron's love went out forever, when I lost my husband, I lost everything that held my life together. Without him, what do I do? Ron was the heart that beats within my heart. My love for Ron still flows through my veins, even today; actually, especially today.

"But I fear that eventually, without Ron in my life, only blood will flow through my veins. I know that my heart will keep beating. But it is an empty heart. It won't beat a little faster when I see Ron, because we won't be together again—not in this world. In this world, this 'sudden vacuum' in my life has left me hollow inside, an empty shell. We are, after all, just a body made of dust, held together by God's will. I still live. I still go places. I still do things. But without a heart, it's not living; it's biology.

"I used to know great, great love. It will take the rest of my life to try to adjust to its loss. I don't know if God will give me enough years to adjust; maybe God will have mercy on a heartbroken widow and reunite us sooner than expected. Sometimes I think of the Gladys Knight and the Pips song where they sing, 'I'd rather live in his world than live without him in mine.' Were it possible, I would eagerly embrace that exchange. The moment I heard of Ron's death was, for me, a moment that will last forever.

"Last night, before going to sleep, I took some comfort in reading something from Ron's fifth book, his autobiography, *Failure to Conform: My Life as an Individual, Apart from the Crowd*. What I want to read to you now is something Ron wrote right after his mother died. It's called 'Sudden Vacuum.'

Sometimes death bulldozes its way into your life uninvited and forcefully takes over. Heartlessly, it proceeds to take a large bite out of your beating heart; though not always unexpected, it nevertheless takes you by surprise. Regardless of how prepared you think you are, you're never ready.

This is the sudden vacuum in your life. The passing of someone you love so dearly. The shock that you feel and feel although you're too numb to feel. Time stands still, momentarily, as you float, adrift, falling, trying to reach out and take their hand and pull them back into your world. The stunned numbness that you feel leaves you too unfocused to process what has just happened, especially if you are there when it happens.

Following the death of someone you love, in this sudden vacuum, the universe somehow, callously, reorganizes itself to adjust to this sudden void—imperceptible to some, an emotional tsunami to others—as love explodes out of your life, while your soul implodes in on itself, creating yet another vacuum.

Life goes on, as they say, just not right away. Time takes time to perform its miracles. Healing? Well, yes, in the fullness of time. We still need space to connect and reconnect. Unwilling to let go, we look at old photos, remembering events we shared. And we savor those sweet memories. We can take some small solace that we're allowed to keep the photos and the memories and the enduring love immortal in our hearts.

In time, we may learn to forgive life for this horrible theft, for all it has taken from us. Just not right away. Each of us carries our individual pain for this great loss. Each of us expresses the collective pain of our combined loss. In doing so, we reaffirm our individual and collective love so that it will travel to our dearly departed loved one.

Then, each of us, in our own way, in our individual lives, will do the best we can to move on. Just not right away.

Grace swallowed hard before continuing.

"Ron was the love of my life. He was the sunshine on my face, the loving hug that never ends. Ron was my firm foundation. He gave me the strength, the encouragement, and the confidence to fully evolve, to reach my full potential in this life. Today, as I stand here before you, it is not on my wobbly knees that I stand. It is on Ron's strong shoulders. Ron's strength is still helping me. It is Ron's love that makes it possible for me to find the words to express the inexpressible.

"Together, Ron and I shared a love that defined a lifetime. I know we will continue to love each other, until eternity dies of old age. Still, with the loss of the reason for my life, I wonder if I can go on, or even if I want to. I know my life will still be filled with two beautiful children, my family, my incredibly loving friend Sally, Ron's books, and a lifetime of so many, many loving memories. But with the dimming of the sunshine on my face, my life is left in a permanent solar eclipse. What can you write when all the words you know run out? I wrote this: 'So great a love, so sweet a dream, so dark the night, so far the fall: A Saturday, a sadder day, the saddest day'—the day I buried my beloved husband.

"You've all probably noticed that I'm not so much speaking about Ron and his life. That is because while I can intellectually accept that the love of my life is gone as a fact, I cannot accept it emotionally, as a reality. I guess that is part of the stages of grief. I still have a long ways to go. People say that life goes on. Well, let it. Life can do whatever it wants. And it can just send me a postcard. Bon voyage!

"I am fully aware of who I am, where I am, and what I feel. I am not detached from the reality of everything that is going on around me. But I don't know how to get past the agony of having my heart ripped out of my life. I can't look at myself in the mirror. I just can't stand to see the pain in my own eyes. You all probably see it too.

"And yes, I know my family and all the people who love me will worry about my health, especially my mental health. I know all that. I also know that this eulogy isn't what you expected. And I know I might repeat myself. I am trying to come to terms with this loss even as I stand before you. How do you live without love when love is the air you breathe? Someone said, 'Love liberates; it does not bind.' Well, I guess I just haven't evolved enough to be at that place yet.

"My heart asked to be buried with him, and so it was, because I can't bear for our hearts to be separated. I know I cannot live without my heart. I am closely watched by a clock that ticks a crooked tick. It measures the time I have left before I can see Ron again, in heaven. That is what my life has become."

Even as she gave voice to her lament, she felt something shift inside her, almost as if Ron were there, touching her shoulder. She remembered the psychic and the message she had brought to Grace and realized she had been carrying that message in her heart all along. Perhaps the ticking clock was not a solemn omen, counting down; perhaps it was a signal to hope and look to the future.

She lifted her head higher. "Yet as I face this whole grieving process, I have already learned a very important, universal, and timeless truth: Love doesn't end; love transcends life, to a higher level of loving, beyond the reach of our reasoning and our logic. And that truth has subconsciously gotten me through each pain-filled day, even as my family and friends have been the ones physically pulling me along and supporting me. Knowing that Ron and I will be reunited in this higher level of loving strengthens me and keeps me moving forward through the despair that surrounds and clings to me.

"I think dying without goodbye-ing is what makes the pain so much more intense. When I left for a doctor's appointment the morning Ron died, I certainly did not realize I had received the final 'I love you' I would ever get from him. I learned a hard lesson in a very hard way, and I want to share that lesson with you. You never know if or when you will see your loved one again. So treasure every

'I love you.' Say, 'I love you' to everyone you love while you can.

"In the past days, so many people—my family, my friends, and my acquaintances—have given me such warm, loving, heartfelt hugs and kisses and silent eyes filled with a language far beyond words. This love has been the only place where I have been able to escape from my pain. Please, please, everyone, we all have to watch over each other and love one another, and let it show.

"Thank you so much for coming today. I love you all so, so much. Please remember to love each other too, and let it show; please, let it show. Thank all of you for being here for my family, and for me. Until next we meet."

Grace returned to her seat on far stronger legs than she began with.

On her journey back to her pew, she saw that men and women alike were crying. Everyone was a bit stunned. They had never experienced anything so visceral and emotionally compelling at a funeral. They probably would have given her a standing ovation if it were appropriate—and if they weren't so drained by Grace's outpouring of love for Ron and the enormous pain she was feeling, and would continue to feel.

Ryder, Melody, and Sally pulled her into another warm, loving group hug. Her children held no anxiety or sadness over Grace's admission that she didn't feel she had anything to live for. Intellectually, they all knew they had each other, but with such an unfathomable chasm opened in their lives, their emotions wouldn't let them see the way past it—yet.

Molly, Jerry, and Frank made their way over to join the hug.

Molly said, "Grace. Beautiful, loving Grace. You've made us so proud and so happy for what you two shared; or as happy as one can be at the funeral of a brother."

Tears flowed freely throughout the church. A number of people in the pews had their own group hugs. Eventually, everyone got back to their seats and sat down.

Father Jerry wept amid an immense swell of empathy, love, pride, and tremendous respect for his beloved friend Grace. He took a long moment to compose himself before returning to the pulpit, still trying to turn off the faucets of his eyes.

He simply said, "Thank you, Grace, for such an incredibly moving statement. The most memorable I've ever heard. And I'm sure everyone here feels the same.

"Ladies and gentlemen, there is little left for me to do but to invite everyone who wishes to, to attend the burial at the cemetery right after this service. Thank you for attending this celebration of the life of our dear departed brother, Ronald James Butler. God bless you all. And as Grace said, everyone, please, love one another and let it show."

Now was the time for the funeral parlor to take over the service. Who was driving with whom to the cemetery had already been arranged. As the coffin was loaded into the hearse, the people in the church started to trickle outside. The friends who attended the funeral made clear to Grace's family, in a very loving way, that they all felt that the burial should be for family alone.

Outside, Ryder spoke with Melody in hushed tones.

"Do you still think that Mom is doing okay after what she said?"

"Yes, Rye. I think Mom is incredibly strong and resilient. In fact, if it is even possible, I have more respect and admiration for her now than I ever did. She's absolutely amazing. I hope I grow up to be her, or at least to be as strong as she is. But we should still speak to Father Jerry to ask him to discreetly see if he can get Mom some professional help—maybe from a sensitive therapist experienced in the loss of a spouse, especially in older couples with longer marriages."

They decided to work their way over to Father Jerry after their duties and obligations had been carried out.

CHAPTER 11

BURIAL

Grace, Ryder, Melody, and Sally were the last ones to leave the church. They said their farewells to those who wouldn't be going to the cemetery for the burial.

Only the hearse, a flower car, Father Jerry's car, and two other cars carrying family members drove out to the cemetery. Father Jerry would leave as early as was appropriate to get back to his other priestly responsibilities.

The hearse and the flower car arrived first. The funeral director had his staff move the casket and the flowers to the grave site. The others followed the casket to the plot on foot. Everyone was silent. There were no chairs. The ceremony would be relatively brief.

Father Jerry stood behind the coffin, facing everyone, and began the service.

There was little left to say to the family now. Mostly what he wanted to do was bring a proper end to this ceremony and allow the family to begin mourning properly.

Father Jerry began, "We are here to say our farewells to our dear departed loved one, Ronald James Butler, a man who loved greatly and was greatly loved in return. So much was said so exquisitely, so beautifully, and so lovingly at Ron's service. Ron's enduring legacy will be in his books, his life, his children, his wife, his many friends, his readers, and the incredible love they all shared. And in time, by the grace of God, there may be grandchildren and great-grandchildren to carry Ron's and Grace's immortality into future generations."

Father Jerry continued, "I was just thinking about something Grace said in her amazing eulogy—that love doesn't end but rather transcends to an even higher, more evolved level of loving. It reminds me of a passage in John, chapter 11, verse 25. Jesus Christ said, 'I am the resurrection and the life. He that believeth in me, though he were dead, yet shall he live; and whosoever liveth and believe in me, shall never die.'"

Churning with emotion and struggling for words, Father Jerry spoke the final words of the service: "In the sure and certain hope of the resurrection to eternal life through our Lord, Jesus Christ, we commend to Almighty God our brother Ronald James Butler, and we commit his body to the ground; earth to earth, ashes to ashes, dust to dust. Lord bless him and keep him.

"Let each of us pray a silent prayer in remembrance and love for Ron. And please continue to keep Ron in your prayers, as I will keep him in mine.

"Now please take one of these red roses and place it on Ron's casket as you pass by, as one final act of love. God bless and keep you all."

Father Jerry was the first to place a rose on Ron's coffin. Molly, Jerry, and Frank came next, then Sally, Ryder, and Melody. Melody and Ryder helped their mother approach the casket, each gently supporting an arm to lend her strength. With a final kiss on a rose petal, Grace laid the final red rose on her beloved's casket. The unbearable pain on Grace's face even prompted tears from the burial crew.

Their own tears becoming waterfalls of great sorrow, Ryder and Melody were determined to stand there, supporting their mother, for as long as she needed.

Finally, Grace turned away from the casket. Melody and Ryder helped her walk toward the exit and to the rest of her family.

Overwhelmed with love and grief, they all surrounded Grace for another group hug of love. After a time, Ron's brothers took their sister by the hand and walked her slowly, reluctantly, to the car.

Sally, still hugging Grace, said, "Molly wanted to remind us that we'll be going over to Angelo's for a meal. We will see them there. Then we can begin the slow process of trying to reconstruct ourselves and our lives."

The four of them made their way to the car. Ryder and Melody asked Sally to take care of Mom for a moment so they could speak with Father Jerry.

Ryder and Melody approached the priest just as he was about to get into his car.

"Father Jerry, can we speak to you for a minute?" Melody asked.

"Of course," he replied, taking her hand in both of his.

She took a deep breath. "You heard and saw how Mom is; we're very worried about her health and her state of mind. We have to go back to college in a few days, and we were hoping you would keep an eye on her. And more than that, we hope she might be willing to get some therapeutic counseling from someone who is experienced with people who have just lost the love of their life."

Father Jerry answered, "It is so like you both to be so loving. Yes, I share your concerns for her health and well-being. In fact, I asked a friend of mine, a psychiatrist, to attend Ron's funeral so that she could learn more about Grace. I have to leave now to speak with her. I will be in touch and let you know how things go. God bless you both."

With that said, Ryder and Melody headed back to the car. Melody drove this time, over to Angelo's. When they arrived, Grace was the last to get out.

Sally helped her stand and said, "Now, Grace dear, we've gotten through the first parts of this incredibly, unbearably difficult process. With all of our duties and obligations carried out, each of us must find our way back to our lives."

Sally understood better than most what Grace was experiencing and knew her friend would need incalculable time to find herself again, but she didn't want Grace to get lost in her grief. A little nudge was in order.

"But we need your love and leadership to help get us there, Grace. Molly, Jerry, Frank, your children . . . and me—with all the Lord has asked you to endure this week, you need to help us all move on from this. Of course, we will also help you, as we are able, but you have to be the tower of strength. Because God has given you that strength, Grace. I could see it when you were up on that pulpit. Maybe you thought you were exposing your weaknesses, but what we saw was strength."

In tears again, Grace gripped Sally's hands tightly, and yet again their eyes said what their mouths could not. At first the twins were a little taken aback that Sally was putting this pressure on their mother, but as they saw Grace's spine straighten, they realized how necessary this step was.

"Now, let's go inside and have some lunch. Afterward, when Molly, Jerry, and Frank head home, we can go over to my house to relax as best we can. I've prepared a dinner for later, if we're hungry. But first, let's get through this lunch and take care of family, okay?"

Grace nodded. "Okay, Sally, let's do this."

Sally took Grace by the arm, and they walked into Angelo's. Melody and Ryder's respect, admiration, and love for Sally doubled, then doubled once more.

Ron's siblings were already seated and motioned to their family to join them. After another round of hugs, tears, and kisses, everyone sat to take a look at their menus. Any distraction from their misery was a good distraction, so they took their time. Then Molly reminded them that everything was already paid for and they could order whatever they wanted. This led to a much closer review of the menu. Amazingly enough, everyone managed to order while there was still daylight.

For a while, no one knew what to say. As usual, Sally rode to the rescue.

"I remember eating here about six months ago with Ron and Grace. Ron always ordered the lasagna, every time. And he especially loved the tiramisu."

Grace just nodded and smiled.

Sally added, "Ron always got a pound of Italian cookies and a box of cannoli to take home. And everything tasted so good; remember that? What do you order for dinner, Grace?"

"I always get the chicken parmesan. I ordered it again tonight."

Melody chimed in, "Rye and I both ordered the chicken parmesan, too, because you always raved about it."

Sally asked Molly, Jerry, and Frank what they ordered. Molly had ordered the spaghetti and meatballs, and Jerry and Frank both ordered the spaghetti with extra-hot sausages.

Molly asked, "Did you both order the extra-hot sausages because you're such macho tough guys?"

Frank pretended to be offended and then answered with a smile, "Nah, we just like the taste."

Jerry added, "And the extra heat doesn't bother us. But you definitely shouldn't order it. Sausages this hot would set your teeth on fire before you could even bite into them."

"Yeah, we know your track record, Molly," Frank added.

By now, everyone was chuckling. A slight "boys against the girls" atmosphere seemed to be developing. Sally's plan to lighten the mood had worked perfectly. And, knowing what she was doing, the others were grateful to her. She had carried each and every one of them this week.

When the food arrived, the family busied themselves with their meals. Molly's brothers, being brothers, each inevitably offered Molly one of their extra, extra-hot sausages, which of course she didn't want.

Ryder thoughtfully offered Molly his glass of water. "You can either drink the water after eating the sausage or dip the sausage in the water before you eat it; your choice."

The gals were getting more and more irritated in a comical way, but everyone was laughing. That was the plan. They had cried earlier and they laughed later, and they all experienced the same release. That made it possible to imagine beginning to live again—and made parting from one another a little easier.

CHAPTER 12

BACK HOME

Ryder drove everyone back to his mom's house, and after relaxing for a few hours, they walked across the lawn to Sally's house. The rain had stopped, and the sky was starting to clear up. Through all the clouds, they could almost see a star or two.

At Sally's house, Sally asked Ryder to help her in the kitchen, giving Melody and Grace a few moments together so that Melody could assess her mom's state of mind. Melody also had a lot to tell her.

"Mom, I want you to know how proud I am. I have such awe and respect for you. I even told Rye and Sally that I want to grow up to be just like you someday. I know I've got a long way to go and so much to learn before I can reach the summit that you're on. I also want to thank you. Your strength, your wisdom, and your fortitude carried all of us through this week. I love you so much, Mom."

They shared a long, warm hug.

Grace was touched but wasn't confident she'd earned her daughter's praise. "Melody. My beautiful, loving Melody. I'm not sure if I can get myself through this excruciating ordeal, much less everyone else."

Melody answered, "Ma, you don't understand; you've already gotten us through this. Now we're just worried about you. You've been under such a tremendous strain, and you're facing an uncertain future. Please don't be afraid to ask for help. Really, Mom. Please love us enough to let us return to you the love you have given us. We need this. Please let us love you this way!

"We will do all that is possible—even impossible—to help you, Mom. Remember, Sally is next door. Father Jerry is a phone call away and as close as the church. And Rye and I can drive here from LA to see you anytime you need us. But you may need more help, Mom, professional help, maybe bereavement counseling, maybe more. Father Jerry can help you with that. Talk to him, Mom."

Grace gazed at her daughter with great pride and said, "I will do all you suggested and more, baby. I love you so much. I'm so very proud of you. I'm sure Dad is in heaven, buffing his fingernails and telling everyone, 'Yep, that's my daughter, all right. Isn't she fantastic?'"

Mother and daughter melted into another long hug. Ryder interrupted this lovefest to announce that dinner was ready and smiled on his way back to the dining room. He knew right then that everything would be okay.

Sally brought out the main course, which was relatively light, and everybody dug in. They had picked at their lunches, but their appetites were starting to return. Eating a meal together brought them another step closer to the stability and normalcy this family desperately needed.

As usual, Sally began the discussion, acknowledging everything they'd been through in the last few days. She wanted to make clear that they'd survived the initial emotional earthquake.

"We did everything we had to do, in just the right way. We went above and beyond above and beyond. We took care of each other and everybody else. I think Ron would be pleased and honored by how everything came together. And that is a tribute to Ron and the love and respect everyone felt for him. Each of us has our own heartache to work through. And Grace has the heaviest burden to carry.

"We must all help one another as much as we can, but we will grieve in our own ways, on our own timetables. I know I still grieve every day for Owen. I just want to add that the three of you did a wonderful job speaking at Ron's funeral. I don't know how you did it. I was not able to do it at Owen's funeral. I don't have the enormous strength you have. You all have so very much to be proud of."

Melody and Ryder rose to give Sally another hug.

Melody said, "Aunt Sally, you're incalculably wise, thoughtful, empathetic, and so boundlessly, so incredibly loving. You're stronger than you think. I don't think you understand how immensely everyone loves and reveres you. You cared for and carried Mom so that she could be strong too. You managed all that needed to be done, and you guided us through this. You are this family's angel."

Ryder added, "Aunt Sally, if you weren't here to make everything work, none of us would've made it through this. When we were in the worst shape of our lives, you strengthened us, organized and managed us, and, most importantly, carried us over the finish line. We did everything we needed to do, and we did it exceedingly well. We got through it, and now we're having dinner at home. That is absolutely amazing, and we have you to thank for it."

Grace was silent for a moment before she summoned the wherewithal to speak.

"Sally, what more can I add to what my profoundly intelligent and wise children have said? You showed us a light at the end of this tunnel of misery. You were 'super mommy' for all of us, especially me. You made us laugh when what we most needed was to laugh. You are the miracle we've needed. As Melody said, you are this family's angel."

Yep, group hug.

Following the "after the ordeal" dinner, they lounged around Sally's living room, drank some decaf coffee, and talked. More laughter and normalcy trickled into their lives, and more pain evaporated with the laughter.

After a while, they realized it was almost tomorrow.

Sally announced, "It's been such a stressful, endless day of responsibilities and grief. We all need some really good sleep. Let's see each other tomorrow for breakfast. The weatherman has finally forecasted a warm, sunny day. Maybe everything can begin to dry out around here, and we can have a leisurely Sunday after all we've been through. We sure as hell need it.

"So this is my polite, very ladylike way of saying, 'Go home, everybody. Let an old lady get some sleep!'"

Sally's speech was convincing. Her house immediately filled with contagious yawning and pre-sleep eye rubbing. They were too tired even for a serious group hug. Just two pecks on the cheek for each of them. They practically had to crawl back home and pull themselves upstairs using both hands and somehow managed to stumble off to their beds, "to sleep, perchance to collapse." (Apologies to Shakespeare.)

CHAPTER 13

SALLY'S RUDE AWAKENING

As forecasted, bright sunshine shone through the windows early Sunday morning, but no one was awake to notice it. They had all earned the right to sleep late, very late.

Grace was awake first. She put the TV on. But just because she was awake and watching Sunday-morning TV didn't mean she was "*up*" up. Not awake enough to make breakfast. She would have stayed in bed for another three hours if she hadn't needed to go to the bathroom.

Melody and Ryder were another case completely. Ryder's TV was still on from the night before, though he slept soundly. Ladylike Melody's TV was off. But then again, so was Melody, chained to a rock in the Land of Nod. You couldn't get her out of bed without a court order, a crowbar, and a ton of dynamite. (Make that two tons.) Were you to flip Melody's bed upside down, gravity itself couldn't have pulled her out.

Maybe gravity combined with explosives?

Luckily for this house, Sally, a former Marine Corps drill instructor, still had her bugle, her metal civil defense hat, a metal garbage can, and a hammer to wake the troops. And Sally had one more thing: a mission. And that was to wake up her platoon and get them downstairs to the mess hall for breakfast, using whatever decibel level she felt was needed.

Sally marched upstairs to the bedrooms and blew Reveille, then lowered her bugle.

Pacing outside the kids' bedrooms, she banged that garbage can with her hammer for all she was worth, playing the "raise the dead" chorus. Grace ran out of her bedroom in a brief panic and then fell on the floor, laughing her cute little drumsticks off. *Sally is indeed wise*, she thought once she'd gotten ahold of herself.

Melody and Ryder were in shock as they bolted out of their bedrooms, crashed into each other, and fell down. *Mission accomplished!* Sally thought with satisfaction as everyone rolled around, overtaken by belly laughs.

Grace announced she would pin a medal on Sally's chest for extraordinary action under fire.

Melody said, "I'll get a bobby pin. Ma, you get a bright-colored ribbon. Rye, you get dressed."

Sally went downstairs to make breakfast. Yep, she was on KP duty again. While she cooked, she hummed the tune for mess call. The last time she had made breakfast for the troops, she made pancakes. Today she would make sausages, bacon, eggs, and toast to celebrate this beautiful day.

Grace, Melody, and Ryder stumbled down to breakfast somehow, all looking like they had been on a twenty-mile hike with fifty-pound backpacks, marching uphill both ways. They each gave Sally a military salute.

"Private Ryder reporting for mess call, sir."

"At ease, mister."

Melody added, "Thank you for the wonderful wake-up, Sally the rooster."

"Thanks for breakfast, Mom," Grace said. At Sally's amused grimace, she added, "It's okay, Sally; I'll get back to being Mom again soon. I'm just enjoying being one of the kids."

All three children laughed.

Sally gave them her best scowl. "Okay, you mugs, how do you want your eggs?"

"Aunt Sally, you are a diabolical mastermind, with such a demented sense of humor. I truly admire that quality in you."

Everybody enjoyed a pleasant, lingering meal, just the four of them. Nobody wanted breakfast to end. Sunshine streamed into the room from every direction. The breakfast dishes would wait for later. Maybe one more cup of coffee all around.

As she finished her breakfast, Grace jumped up with a frightened start. Something had touched her.

"What's the matter?" Sally demanded.

Grace stared down at the intruder with a very strange look on her face. The answer came in the form of a meow. Moonbeam jumped up on Grace's lap. Famished, she started to lick the eggs off all the plates.

All four of them sat stunned by Moonbeam's return. It slowly dawned on them that the cat had never actually left the house. She must have been hiding somewhere inside all the while. There had been no reason to go out in the thunderstorm and the windstorm. There was no cat to rescue. Ron died for nothing.

The cruel injustice of it all emerged in surges of anger, frustration, tears, and indigestion. Would this intensity be directed at Moonbeam, the cause of it all? She could probably have used a life insurance policy right about then.

The humans all stared at each other, thinking the same bitter thoughts: *What is the point? What is the lesson from all this? How could God allow this cruelty and injustice to happen?*

They couldn't find the answer in each other's eyes.

Melody and Ryder helped their mother to bed. Then they returned to their beds. There was nothing for Sally to do but put the breakfast dishes and cookware in the sink and go home, perhaps to her own bed.

But before she left, Sally gave Moonbeam a large breakfast and plenty of water.

∾

Time would have to work its wonders, or at least do all it could. Everything was quiet in the house. There was nothing to do but lie in bed and think about everything the family had learned and experienced.

Melody and Ryder were worried about leaving their mom like this. She might even be suicidal, but Melody didn't feel qualified to make that call. With this thought in mind, she phoned Father Jerry. The priest said he would come by this evening to check on Grace and speak with them about her condition. He would ask the psychiatrist he had mentioned to join him.

Melody, Sally, and Ryder knew that Grace wouldn't want to go out; therefore, they would have Father Jerry and the psychiatrist over for dinner. A more informal setting would be less stressful for everybody anyway.

∾

Ryder set the table while Melody and Sally finished up in the kitchen. At 7 p.m., right on schedule, Father Jerry and an unfamiliar woman arrived at their door. Father Jerry introduced Dr. Wall to everyone as a psychiatrist. He wanted Grace to know who she was and what field she practiced in. Grace shook Dr. Wall's hand, understanding that the psychiatrist was primarily there for her.

Dr. Wall said, "I have actually seen you before, Grace. Father Jerry asked me to attend your husband's funeral, and your eulogy was very powerful, moving, and incredibly eloquent. It was painful to hear. I can't imagine how painful it was for you to stand up there and deliver it. There was so much anguish, along with a tremendous amount of love, in everything you said. I can just imagine how proud Ron would be of you. I have a tremendous amount of admiration and respect for you, Grace; I really do. I look forward to getting to know you better—getting to know all of you better."

Grace simply said, "Welcome to our home, Dr. Wall. And, of course, you too, Jerry." To Dr. Wall she explained, "Father Jerry and Ron grew up in the same neighborhood and went to school together. He would've been Ron's best man if he weren't needed to perform the ceremony! So I understand why Father Jerry is concerned about me and wants to protect me in every way. And I love him for that. So, Dr. Wall, welcome to our home. We're having roast beef for dinner. I hope that will please you."

Dr. Wall responded, "Thank you so much, Grace, for inviting me."

To take the pressure off, Father Jerry suggested that Grace make time to speak with Dr. Wall next week and that the psychiatrist could arrange for Grace to join her bereavement group as well.

Grace said she was fine with taking these steps. Just not right away. There was much to do even after the funeral and burial. She had to work things out with the insurance company, Social Security, Medicare, the banks, and other matters. And she needed alone time. She could then consider attending a group and seeing a psychiatrist.

Grace had bought herself time to process her grief. At the end of dinner, Father Jerry and Dr. Wall thanked Grace and her family for the warm welcome and a wonderful evening and then headed for their cars.

Everyone was ready for bed after their roller coaster of a day, and each had a great deal to think about and process.

CHAPTER 14

THE PLOT THICKENS

As Grace lay in her bed, much weighed on her mind. Melody and Ryder would be heading back to LA on Tuesday. They had only Monday to spend together as a family and recover.

Then everything would supposedly get back to "normal." *What does any of it mean?* Grace wondered. *Normal, abnormal, left, right, forward, backward. Ron is dead. Never to be seen again. And things will never be the same again. So, what else is new? Ron is dead! Ron is dead!!* She suspected that "normal" meant getting used to the abnormal.

Everyone was trying to cope and adjust the best they could with their pain and grief. And individuals can usually do that, in time. But how would the family group deal with its collective pain? How could they figure out a way that worked for everybody?

Eventually, Grace was blessed with the refuge that sleep provides. In sleep, in dreams, everything isn't only possible; it's likely.

Before sleeping that night, Melody and Ryder had a consult in Ryder's room.

Melody said, "Rye, I don't know how you feel about conspiracy theories, but Sally and Father Jerry are cooking something up. And they're being extra sneaky about it. Sally told me he wants everyone to join him for lunch at the church tomorrow. What do you think those two are planning? I hope it's something funny."

Ryder answered, "I think you're right, Mel. The plot thickens! Now get out of my room; one of us is tired."

Melody responded, "I've been thrown out of better dumps than this! Good night."

∼

On Monday morning, they all arrived at Sally's door. She was whistling suspiciously—suspicious because she never whistled. Everyone wondered what was going on here. Sally wore her best "I know something you don't know" expression.

At about noon, they piled into Sally's car for the short ride to the church. Father Jerry had everything ready to go, just as he and Sally planned. When they entered, Father Jerry welcomed them with a hug. Both he and Sally wore self-satisfied grins, which greatly added to suspicions and anticipation alike. The family's confusion just made it more fun for the coconspirators.

Father Jerry finally said, "Well, everyone, welcome. Let me say first of all that I welcome you here not as Father Williams but as Ron's lifelong best friend, Jerry. And as Ron's lifelong best friend, I know many things about Ron that you guys don't know because you just weren't there; some of you were still in heaven, waiting to be born.

"As best friends, Ron and I shared a lot of adventures long before Grace officially entered the scene as his lady love. Some of our adventures were incredibly funny, some were downright dangerous, and some might be considered either slightly or definitely illegal. Just in case, we are still keeping an eye on the statute of limitations on a couple of them. In my professional opinion as an experienced priest, it was a miracle that we were never arrested! Some of these stories may even shock Grace, putting gray hairs on her ulcers. Of course, these stories won't affect Sally. As we all know, Sally is indestructible.

"Let me start by telling you when Ron and I first met. Well, I suppose we never really *met* each other. It's more that our mothers knew each other as kids, from school and church. They are the ones who actually met. And then Ron and I got pushed alongside each other in strollers on our mothers' walks together. Later on, we went to the same kindergarten and were in public school together through high school and graduation in 1968.

"We were different in many significant ways, yet we had so much in common, too: the stupid 'guy things' we had fun doing, like for 'I dare you' and 'Why not?' reasons." He paused and cleared his throat with a mischievous twinkle in his eye. "I've gotta be careful here. I don't want to tarnish Ron's image in your eyes, not to mention the risk of demeaning my holy stature as a humble, pious priest. And, of course, I also have to maintain a certain amount of plausible deniability. But I couldn't have done my 'stupid guy things' without experienced, expert guidance from my partner in crime, my dear best friend, Ron Butler.

"While I was at seminary school, Ron was in college. He told me some dangerously funny stories about his college years. Some of the guys at college were pissed off at the dean for whatever reason. They hatched some wonderful plots, which you probably won't believe, but here they are. Maybe Ryder and Melody will feel the need to replicate some of these diabolical s schemes at their own colleges? So, here goes.

"First, Ron and two other college friends '*borrowed*' a milk cow from a nearby farm. They took the cow up two flights of stairs to the dean's office so that the dean would have some very fresh milk for his coffee in the morning. The 'udderly' fiendish aspect is that you can get a cow to go upstairs just fine because it can see where it's going. But there's no way in hell you can get the cow to go downstairs when it can't see where it is going. I asked Ron how the dean got the cow out of his office. He said, 'The first to go were the porterhouse steaks, and then the rib eyes. The last to go was the chop meat for the hamburgers.'

"Apparently, the dean wasn't properly pleased with the 'Where's the beef?' gift from his devoted students. And he made his displeasure felt by all the students in the college. Ron and the guys felt that the gauntlet had been thrown, and they accepted the challenge. They all brainstormed on the problem and devised a creative solution to piss off the dean even more.

"It took them some time to accomplish everything, but they were able to move the entire contents of the dean's office—furniture, wall hangings, lamps, the carpet, everything—over to the women's bathroom on the same floor. They were very proud of wedging the dean's couch above the stalls. They also removed the plaque with the dean's title from his door and placed it outside the ladies' bathroom. And then, to keep the balance of the universe, they attached the ladies' room sign on the dean's door. Of course, with this second great achievement, they were *legends*! The dean never found out who the culprits were, but in certain circles, Ron and his college buddies were 'secretly famous.'

"Let me tell you another story that Ron told me. He and his brothers were at somebody's wedding—he couldn't remember whose—and their uncle Zeke was having far too good a time. Now, Uncle Zeke was very proud of his 'walrus handlebar' mustache. It really was a work of art. It took him two years to perfect it; it was his pride and joy. And he twirled it and played with it all night long.

"His three nephews, Ron, Jerry, and Frank, were mesmerized as he pranced around the wedding reception. As was customary with Uncle Zeke, he got falling-down, dead drunk. Two of Zeke's brothers dragged him off to a room away from the crowd to recuperate. Of course, this was of great interest to his nephews, who got the brilliant idea to shave off one half of the magnificent mustache, then scurry away to establish a credible alibi.

"When the wedding reception was winding down, Uncle Zeke's two brothers took him home and got him into bed. With all of them drunk, nobody noticed that he had only half a mustache. Of course, this was riotously funny to Ron and his brothers. They all tried to imagine the look of horror on their uncle's face when he realized that his upper lip was missing something. 'What happened to the rest of my mustache? Oh my God! I've been robbed! All that time, all that work!' Maybe the missing half of his mustache would end up on a milk carton. 'Have you seen this missing half mustache? If you have, call 1-800-UPPERLIP.'

"I can also remember the first time Ron and me got severely drunk. I mean, 'driving the porcelain bus' drunk. And that incident made me believe in conspiracy theories. When Ron and I floated back to our respective homes, we were blitzed! Our parents sent us right to bed. It was only 10 p.m. Saturday, and we were both dead to the world.

"Well, it turned out our parents had called each other earlier to see if we had checked in and were okay. Thus was born an amazing and memorable conspiracy between our two families. My parents and Ron's parents hatched an intricate *Mission Impossible* conspiracy to teach a couple of drunken amateurs a lesson we would never forget.

"The exact same things happened at both our houses. My father came into my bedroom yelling, 'Wake up, Jerry! You were so drunk you slept all day Sunday. It's Monday morning, and we've been calling you for twenty minutes. Are your ears still so drunk that you couldn't hear us? *Wake up, already*!' I stumbled out of bed, still drunk, and got dressed in my school clothes as fast as I could, falling twice just trying to get my pants on. My father kept yelling at me to hurry up. When I carefully lurched down the stairs with two hands on the banister, I wasn't sure if the room was spinning clockwise or counterclockwise. I just wished that it would stop.

"My father was in his suit for work. My sister and brother were heading out the door. My father barked, 'No time for breakfast! You're already very late. The bus just left without you, and you'll have to run to school so you won't be late for class. Remember, you have a test today. I'm sure you spent the whole weekend studying, didn't you, Jerry? Well, I have to go to work now so I won't be late like you.'

"My father left. I started to run to school, even though I felt like I might pass out at any moment. There was no way I could say that

I was too sick to go to school after my parents let me sleep all day Sunday to recover.

"I arrived at school just before Ron. We tried all the school doors, but we couldn't open any of them. *Oh no*, we thought. *All the kids have gone in already, and they locked us out!* We tried banging on all the school doors—no luck. And we both had a test today. What were we going to tell our parents? There was nothing to do but return to our separate homes and face the music.

"When I got home, my whole family was back around the kitchen table, having breakfast. My mother had made her special french toast, which she only made Sunday mornings. She said, 'Sit down, Jerry, have some Sunday-morning breakfast. It's your favorite: french toast.' It finally dawned on me that I hadn't slept all day into Monday morning. My whole family had gotten up very early on Sunday morning, gotten dressed, and gone through the motions just to set me up.

"When they saw that realization on my face, they started to laugh and laugh and laugh. They got me good. And the same thing happened at Ron's house. We certainly learned our lesson. And since that time, Sunday mornings have always been very special for me. Good thing, too!

"That's probably enough stories, but I have what I hope is the only existing photo of one of our more moronic escapades, which, thus far, I have been unwilling to reveal to anyone. This photo, which I will call 'exhibit X' for reasons that will become obvious in the end, provides conclusive proof of just how idiotic a couple of young guys like us can be under the right circumstances.

"This photo was taken while Ron and I and a couple of our high school buddies were doing our 'elbow exercises,' one shot glass at a time, celebrating our high school graduation. And yes, I can confirm that the two a-holes in the photo are Ron Butler and myself. You can tell Ron is the one on the right by the distinctive little dimple 'where the sun don't shine.'" Father Jerry winked at Grace, who couldn't help chuckling past the hand she'd slapped over her mouth. "In this photo, we are both bare-assed naked with celebratory writing on our asses.

"What was written on our delicate little derrieres in capital letters is as follows: On my upper left cheek was a 'G-R.' On my upper right cheek was an 'A-D.' Ron's upper left cheek had a 'U-A,' and his upper right a 'T-E.' Any cheerleaders here see where this is going? Then on my lower left ass cheek was 'CLASS,' and on my lower right cheek was 'OF.' Ron's lower left and right ass cheeks were adorned with '19' and '68,' respectively.

"Of course, that spells 'Graduate class of 1968.' And here is the photo to prove it. I'm just glad they weren't tattoos. Yeah, yeah, laugh your asses off now. You won't laugh so much when I tell you that Ron and I got a million cool points each for our drunken buffoonery, which is half the points you need to get into 'cool heaven'! You see, I knew you would be impressed. 'Cool heaven,' here we come.

"Well, everybody, it's a rare event when the tables are turned and you get to hear the confessions of a priest. But today you have. Lucky!"

After his audience had somewhat settled down after collapsing with laughter, Father Jerry continued, "I don't know if any of you still have an appetite after seeing exhibit X, but we're ready for lunch."

They filed into the rectory dining room, where lunch had already been served. Still laughing at the stories revealed, they got down to eating their meal, taking their time and stretching out the fun time.

Sometime after the meal, Father Jerry and Sally reconvened.

"Sally, I learned from you just how important, cathartic, therapeutic, and healing laughter can be. I hope these stories help all of us. Thanks again. You really are a walking, talking miracle unto yourself. Thank God for you."

Ryder and Melody assured Father Jerry that the resurrection of some of the stunts he and their father had pulled would get serious consideration if anyone earned it at their respective colleges.

Ryder couldn't help asking, "Was exhibit X included in the yearbook?"

Of course, everyone laughed.

Father Jerry, the pious priest, said, "Hell no! I could never have become a Catholic priest with that photo. Thank God there was no Facebook or internet in those days. Mamma mia! The pope would want my head on a silver platter like John the Baptist."

Each family member had relished hearing the unexpectedly hilarious stories about Ron, and they all felt ready for a nap after so much food and laughter. Once home, one by one, they all fell asleep.

CHAPTER 15

A VERY SPECIAL VISITOR

Grace had an extremely vivid dream that afternoon, to the point where it felt like an elevated experience, a vision of sorts.

Ron appeared, dressed in white, only visible from his chest up. He murmured to the sleeping Grace, "Grace, my love, it's Ron. Please speak with me."

Grace became restless in her bed, halfway between sleep and wakefulness.

"Speak with me, my love."

Grace answered, "Ron, is that you? How is this possible?" She immediately realized she didn't care how it was possible. "Oh, I just want to hold you and kiss you. I need you. I can't do this all alone."

Ron said, "This is all I'm allowed to do, my love. I can't come to you physically, in an awakened state; I just can't. It's not possible. But I'm here with you now, my love. I'm here for you. This is what the power of our love and God's grace makes possible for us. As the psychic told you, love doesn't end; it transcends."

Crying in her sleep, Grace said, "Ron, I need you. I can't go on without you. How can we go on apart from each other? It's not fair! How can I be with you, Ron? How can I hold you? What do I have to do?"

Ron answered, "Grace, the love we share makes it possible for us to be together as we are right now—in the only possible way for us to be together. Nothing else can be done. I've tried and tried, Grace. And, my love, you have very important work to do here, where you are right now. You have to take care of Ryder, Melody, Sally, my brothers and sister—and yourself. You have to take care of you too. That's all I'm allowed to say, Grace. Please trust me on this."

Through a flood of tears, Grace finally nodded. She then sank into a deeper, more restorative sleep, resting soundly for many hours.

That night, Melody and Ryder prepared a wonderful dinner for Grace and Sally in gratitude and respect for all they'd been through and overcome. Sally would be over in about ten minutes; meanwhile, Melody went upstairs to check on her mom, who was still asleep. But something in the room felt strange. A little alarmed at her mother's stillness, Melody placed her hand on the sleeping woman's shoulder.

Grace responded, "Five more minutes, Ron. Just five more minutes."

Melody shook her mom's shoulder slightly.

"Okay, Ron, I'll be up in a minute!" Grace groused.

Melody said firmly, "Mom. Wake up, Mom. It's me, Melody."

When Grace opened her eyes, she was surprised to see her daughter.

"Oh, Melody, it's you. I thought you were Ron poking me to wake up again. I'm awake now. What time is it?"

"It's 7 p.m. Dinner is on the table. Sally is on her way over."

"Okay, Mel, I'll be right down."

Melody responded uncertainly, "Okay, Mom."

She headed down to the dining room and told Ryder, "Mom was acting weird when she woke up. She called me Ron. She thought I was Dad."

Ryder responded, "That doesn't sound so weird. It seems pretty normal that she would be dreaming about Dad. I've dreamed about him too."

"I suppose you're right."

Sally arrived for dinner and asked how Grace was doing before speaking another word. Melody only said that she was on her way down for dinner, not wanting to put more pressure on Sally after everything she had done for them that week.

When Grace arrived for dinner a few minutes later and they all sat to eat, Sally sensed something was going on. She didn't say anything immediately, just noting the concern on the twins' faces.

After dinner, Sally served cups of decaf coffee and said, "So, did everyone have a restful nap? I certainly did."

"Yeah, I think it helped a lot," Ryder said.

"Me too," Melody added, glancing at Grace. "Restful."

"How about you, Grace? How was your nap?"

As if waiting to be asked, Grace eagerly clasped her hands under a bright smile.

"Sally, I had such an amazing sleep," she gushed. "Ron came to speak with me. He proved to me exactly what the psychic told me and what I've kept repeating to myself: that love doesn't end. It really does transcend death. I know now that he cannot be with me, and I cannot be with him—and that is okay.

"Let me put it this way: do you guys remember the movie *Ghost* with Demi Moore and Patrick Swayze? Do you remember the sequence where Demi Moore was at the pottery wheel and her late husband came to her, and they had that wonderful, incredibly romantic, incredibly loving scene? Well, it's not exactly the same as the movie, but the feeling was pretty much the same, just without that great Righteous Brothers song.

"Ron told me that I have important work to do here. That is my fate. But because we shared and still share such an amazing, magical love between us, we have been blessed with the likelihood of more of these contacts. I feel that if I really need him, he will find a way to come to me in my sleep, and we can be together on that level. I think that is such a wonderful blessing from God. Don't you all agree?"

The others were a little hesitant to answer. Sure, Ron might have visited her in her sleep. More likely, she had a lovely dream about him. But did it matter what she believed if the dream made her happy? Was there a difference between true spirits and lost loved ones seen in dreams? Still, it was disconcerting that Grace immediately took the experience as a fantastical visitation.

Sally answered, "Grace, you are indeed blessed to have such a miraculous encounter. I'm happy for you. And I'm sure the twins feel the same, don't you?"

Melody and Ryder just nodded. Grace was all smiles. Though concerned, her family was grateful that she seemed more lighthearted than the day before and that they were again enjoying the normalcy of having dinner together as a family.

After dinner, Sally said, "Well, everyone, I know Billy will be here early in the morning to drive you two to the airport. And I know you have a lot of packing to do. So, don't let us keep you. Say good night to your mom. Good night, kids."

Melody and Ryder kissed Sally and Grace and went upstairs to pack, leaving the two friends alone in the dining room.

Sally told Grace, "I don't really understand your encounter with Ron. But I am happy for you, and I do think that it is a blessing. And who deserves that more than you?" She gave Grace a warm, loving hug before heading home. "See you in the morning, dear."

Grace hugged her coffee cup for a moment, and then she and Moonbeam went upstairs.

The sounds of Melody and Ryder packing for their trip back to LA reassured her. Things seem to be returning to an old, familiar routine. But without Ron, what did being all alone mean now? She had lost solitude and found aloneness. How the hell was she going to adjust?

With that thought on her mind, Grace went to bed, hoping for but not expecting sleep after her long nap, and uncertain of what the night had planned for her.

∼

Billy arrived around 6:30 a.m. to take Ryder and Melody to the airport. He was just in time for breakfast. Afterward, he loaded the luggage as Melody and Ryder gave their mom a hug and kiss goodbye. They had to trust that God, Sally, and Father Jerry would take care of her. Plus, Sally would give them updates, and they always had email and phones.

With the kids were on their way to the airport and back to school, Grace was all alone in the house, just herself and Moonbeam, who had found her mommy and curled up in her fluffy robe. This sudden solitude came as a relief, but she sensed that wouldn't last. Solitude is wonderful and comforting when there is an end in sight—simply some time to spend with yourself, knowing that the bustle of life can be returned to at any moment.

Solitude is frightening and painful when it becomes aloneness, and when having known what it is not to be alone makes the aloneness so very crushing.

CHAPTER 16

SOLITUDE

When the doorbell rang, Grace realized she had been asleep for about three hours. Grace put Moonbeam on the floor and went to the door. To her surprise, it was the psychic medium.

"Please, come in," Grace said in her most welcoming voice. "It is wonderful to see you again, Ms. . . . I'm sorry; you didn't give your name."

"Thank you again, Mrs. Butler," the medium replied as she walked in. When Grace gestured toward the kitchen, the woman shook her head briefly with a smile. "My name is Angela. I believe we'll likely see more of each other, so true introductions are warranted. I'm here again for an important reason, and yes, it relates to Ron. I know that he came to you in your sleep. I'm here to answer any questions you may have in this regard. By the way, your reference to the movie *Ghost* was a wonderful way to explain Ron's 'visit.' I think it gave your family a frame of reference that helped them better understand and reassured them that you were okay.

"I want to confirm what Ron already told you and what you already reasoned out for yourself. Ron can come to you again under the proper circumstances. And he can come to you when you really need him, and he will know when you do.

"And I will know those times too. I can come to you in this realm of existence when necessary. Remember, Grace, as Ron has already told you, there is no possible way for you to be with him. You have vital work to do here, so here is where you must remain. The work you have to do is something you already know in the back of your mind. But things will become much clearer to you in the fullness of time.

"Grace, you're dealing with a great deal of turmoil. Much is beyond the reach of your reasoning and your imagination. I'm here to help you learn to be an 'accepter.' There are things you cannot control and cannot understand, yet they are. You must evolve to a higher level and learn to accept these things."

She gripped Grace's hands tightly and held her gaze for a good long while, almost to the point where Grace grew uncomfortable—yet there was something in Angela's eyes that soothed her and made her accept what the psychic was saying.

Finally, Angela concluded, "With that said, I must take my leave. I have more work to do. It was good to speak with you again, Grace. Go with God."

Angela strode right back out the door without letting Grace get a word in edgewise. Grace was once again left stunned in her wake, feeling like she'd suffered intellectual whiplash. *What is real and what is not, and what is going on, and what am I supposed to do—or not do?*

Her head still spinning, she heard the phone ring. She was startled to hear Father Jerry's voice. He was calling to check on her.

"Well, Ryder and Melody left earlier this morning for school. I'm enjoying a quiet morning with just me and Moonbeam. Sally is giving herself much-needed, well-deserved time to sleep late for a change. So, everything is okay here. How are you?"

Father Jerry said, "Grace, I'm not calling to check on the twins or on Sally. I know they're okay. I'm concerned about you and how you're doing." He cleared his throat and said more gently, "I know Ron came to you and Angela stopped by. Don't ask how I know; I just do. So, as your priest and especially your friend, I wanted to see how *you* are doing. Are you doing okay, Grace?"

After a few moments of thoughtful silence, Grace replied, "I am in tremendous pain, and I am confused about a great many things, but I'm really doing okay."

Father Jerry said, "Grace, my dear friend, I do know how much pain you're in, and I understand why you would be confused. That is a great reason to speak with Dr. Wall. You've been through so much in a short period. Someone experienced in this area can help you make sense of all of this. I took the liberty of making an appointment for you with Dr. Wall next Tuesday at eleven, if that works for you. Or we can reschedule to a more convenient time of your choosing."

Far from being upset, Grace was grateful not to have to decide if she was up for this experience yet. "Thank you, Jerry. Tuesday morning will be fine. Actually, I'm looking forward to speaking with her. You've been so helpful to me and my family. I don't know how to thank you. Thank God for you. You are a blessing to all of us, my dear, dear friend."

"You are very welcome, Grace. Remember, I'm here for you whenever you need me. If you want to talk, we'll talk. If you need to see me, I'm here. And of course, Sally lives just next door. Go with God, Grace. Be well. And let me know how things go with Dr. Wall."

As she concluded her call with Father Jerry, Sally walked into the house without knocking, carrying a bag of fresh bagels. She was a little surprised to see her friend up and about.

"What's up, girl? What's going on?"

Grace shook her head. "You won't believe it. Angela, that psychic medium from last week, came by to speak with me earlier this morning. She already knew about the experience I had with Ron. And she confirmed everything Ron had already told me! And to make things extra weird, Father Jerry just called me, and *he* already knew about my encounter with Ron and my visit from Angela. He also made an appointment with that psychiatrist, Dr. Wall, for next Tuesday. Does he think I'm crazy, or does he know I'm not? I don't know what to think anymore. What do you think of all that, Sally?"

Sally shook her head at the glut of information and said, "I think I need a strong cup of Irish cream coffee and a bagel to wash the coffee down. You probably need one too, Grace."

They continued their conversation in the kitchen, with Moonbeam curled up in Grace's warm lap.

Sally continued, "Grace, I'm not in a position to make much sense of this. Let me just say that I'm happy you have an appointment with Dr. Wall. I think she is your best bet to find the answers you need. Do you want me to go with you?"

Grace rested her chin in her hand. "I think you're right, Sally, about Dr. Wall. And thanks, but no thanks. I'll drive myself over. I have a lot to go over before I see her. You know, Sally, these bagels are delicious."

Moonbeam sniffed Grace's bagel, but she wasn't impressed.

The rest of the day was spent with the three of them on the couch in front of the TV, just watching game shows until the soap operas came on. They fell asleep in front of the soaps, each on one arm of the couch. Everything was getting back to "abnormal" at last.

A few hours later, they both woke with back pains from sleeping at odd angles and decided to call it a day. Sally headed home. A few hours later, it was dark and time for dinner. They spotted each other in their kitchen windows as they prepared their respective dinners in their respective homes. They waved and somehow yawned at the exact same time. This really made them laugh. They motioned to each other, indicating that they were both sleepy and would go right to bed after dinner. Sally gave Grace a thumbs-up.

They waved good night and returned to their lives, each watching a little TV with dinner and then retiring for the night to their beds.

CHAPTER 17

APPOINTMENT WITH DR. WALL

Tuesday morning the following week, Moonbeam the rooster sat on Grace's chest and tapped her gently with her paws. Now would be an excellent time to feed her. And after she was fed, Moonbeam gave Grace permission to head out to her doctor's appointment.

The week after Ron's funeral had been a slog. The days blurred together in a simple cycle of feeding Moonbeam, having breakfast with Sally, and falling asleep in front of the TV on the couch. She hadn't dreamed again about Ron, but she held on to the promise that he would come when she needed him. She suspected she might need him tonight.

As today was Grace's first time driving to Dr. Wall's office, she gave herself extra time to find it. She couldn't help the sense of déjà vu. She had driven to a doctor's office two Tuesdays ago at 11 a.m., the day Ron went in search of Moonbeam and never came home.

She arrived early at the doctor's office, which was actually in Dr. Wall's home. The friendly doctor answered the door at the patient's entrance.

"Grace, it's so wonderful to see you. Welcome, welcome, welcome. Please, sit over here. You'll be shocked to learn that there is a forest's worth of paperwork for you to fill out before we begin. You know how it is: 'Commerce before medicine'!"

"There is nothing more tragic in the universe than a bureaucrat who needs just one more piece of paper."

"Ain't that the truth?" Dr. Wall replied. "So, Grace, I will leave you to fill out the paperwork while I make some tea—or would you prefer coffee?"

Grace answered, "Tea will be fine, thank you, Doctor."

"I'll be back shortly."

About fifteen minutes later, they sat in chairs opposite each other, sipping tea.

Dr. Wall began, "Grace, I know a little about you from Father Williams and seeing you at Ron's funeral and of course the dinner at your home. But I would like to start with you telling me about your children, Melody and Ryder, if you feel comfortable doing so. You must be so proud of them."

Grace replied, "Yes, Doctor, I'm extremely proud of who they are, especially the wonderful values they both demonstrate. It might sound cocky, but I think Ron and I did a wonderful job raising our children. Of course, kids don't arrive with an instruction manual. You have to wing it and hope for the best. Considering everything, I think we both did pretty well. Thank Jesus for that!"

Dr. Wall continued, "Father Williams told me that they are fraternal twins?"

"Yes, Doctor. Believe me; they are not at all identical. Let's see. Ryder is the oldest, born a few minutes before Melody. He states that he has seniority and that it makes all the difference. Melody has somewhat of a different perspective on the matter. She says that just means Ryder will be old long before she will.

"Ryder is highly intelligent. He speaks very fast. Everybody thinks he's from New York or something because of the velocity of his verbiage. I'm surprised he doesn't bite his tongue trying to keep up with his mind. I think he's a little insecure that he might not be completely understood, so he compensates by repeating himself where he feels it's needed or rephrasing what he has already said, which most people find confusing and somewhat irritating.

"Ryder's intelligence is balanced with an absolutely demented sense of humor, just like his father. People find him hard to peg, hard to categorize. He is highly capable and unpredictable. There is an undefinable quality about him. This can sometimes make people feel a little threatened. On the other hand, he is overall respected and well liked because he makes everyone, and I mean everyone, laugh. He says outrageous things that other people just cannot say. Even the most pious people seem to like the reckless abandon of his jokes. Nothing is sacred or off limits to Ryder. That's just the way he is.

"Ryder feels that humor comes from God, so God must have a sense of humor. That is why he created the human race in his own image, for his own amusement. To hear Ryder explain it, the human race was the first reality TV show. What else can I tell you about Ryder? He wants to be a writer, like his dad. Actually, Ron named him Ryder because it sounds like 'writer.'"

Dr. Wall smiled warmly as Grace spoke of her son, then asked about Melody.

The proud mommy responded, "What can I tell you about my beautiful Melody? I can tell you that I named her after my passion, which was my long career as a high school music teacher. Melody is demure, soft, and quiet, most of the time. But she is the one most likely to have the biggest, loudest belly laugh at something Ryder says or does. She is classically beautiful, with an alluring smile and—when she's not cackling at Ryder—an infectious, disarming laugh you can't help but laugh along with. She puts everyone at ease right away. She radiates so much love and goodness that it draws people to her.

"Where Ryder is, at his core, the brooding twin, an introvert, Melody is very much an extrovert. Where Ryder is a thinker, Melody is a 'feeler.' I've always been amazed that two kids with the same parents, growing up in the same household all their lives, can be so radically different from one another, but they are. Only the psychiatric community knows why."

Dr. Wall just continued smiling.

"Where was I? Oh, Melody. Everybody looks forward to seeing Melody and being around her. Her friends and acquaintances talk about her before she arrives. There is a mysterious, wise quality about her that makes people want to tell her their most intimate secrets.

"Of course, Melody usually doesn't want to hear that stuff. It's none of her business, and hearing it makes her very uncomfortable. She doesn't want to carry the burden of their secrets. But somehow, she has become an involuntary secret keeper. I've often joked that she has 'confessional eyes,' and 'confessional ears,' too, because the same things happen on the phone. People tell her the most embarrassing things.

"I told her I would make a sign saying, 'The shingle is out, the doctor is in.' As a joke, Ryder got her a little ceramic figure of Lucy's psychiatry stand from *Peanuts*—you know, 'Lucy's Psychiatric Help 5¢.' Ryder filled the ceramic with twenty nickels."

By now, Grace's chin was in her hands as she shook her head with a grin, marveling over what she and Ron had created. "Those are my kids."

"Thank you, Grace," Dr. Wall murmured. "That does give me a clearer understanding of your children, who are, of course, a major part of your support system."

Grace said, "Yes, they are. It's interesting that you started our session by asking about my children, whom you've already met. I guess having a mother speak about her children is a good way to put me at ease, Doctor?"

"Yes, Grace. And I would love it if you called me by my first name, Judith; however, you may refer to me in the way that makes you most comfortable."

Feeling a little like she had wasted half a session on an icebreaker exercise, Grace sighed and responded, "Okay, Doctor, if you prefer, I can call you Judith. Shall we begin?"

Dr. Wall cocked her head at the sour note in Grace's tone.

"Grace, you sound rather aggressive with me while I am trying to help you. Are you frustrated for some reason?"

The question seemed to uncover a well of frustration within Grace that she hadn't realized existed. She started calmly, but then the emotions flooded forth.

"Well, you see, Doctor—excuse me, Judith—I'm in a great deal of continuous, never-ending agony." She was almost surprised to find that despite the few moments of joy she'd experienced since Ron's death, despite the calm she'd found in her solitude, this statement was true. Ron's visit had numbed the pain; coming back out into the real world was like being doused with a bucket of ice water. "I still need to deal with all the bureaucrats at the insurance company, the IRS, Social Security, Medicare, the banks, and the list goes on forever, which of course adds to my pain.

"So, Dr. Judith, I'm not in the best mood and not in the best shape to delve into even more pain with regard to my husband's death. One week ago to the day, to the minute, I went to a doctor's appointment, and when I got back from that appointment, my husband was gone. I haven't had time to find solid ground again. I thought I was grateful to Father Jerry for making this appointment for me, but now I wonder if I'm not a little resentful, too, that he seems to want me to move on so quickly from something that still very much exists for me."

Grace continued, "Perhaps you think I am emotionally disabled, Doctor. I don't think so. I am deeply focused on the continuing love I still feel for my late husband. You say you heard my eulogy. Intellectually, I know and I have accepted that my husband is dead. However, emotionally, I am still deeply in love with him. How can he be dead when I still love him so much that I can't stand it?"

Dr. Wall solemnly received her words and the anger that filled them. She gave Grace a few moments of silence before responding.

"Well, Grace, I can't remember the author, but a poet once wrote, 'Love can conquer anything, anything at all, except death.'"

The starkness of Dr. Wall's response hit Grace hard.

The emotional dam broke, unleashing an ocean of tears—precisely what Dr. Wall was hoping for. She knelt beside Grace's chair with a box of tissues and held her, letting her cry as much pain out of her system as she could.

There would be many more tears in the coming weeks and months, maybe longer, maybe for as long as Grace lived, but this moment marked significant progress on the road before them. Dr. Wall knew that the best thing she could give Grace right now was this hug and this acceptance of her tears. Grace needed this emotional catharsis more than anything else; and Dr. Wall knew that Grace knew it too.

Eventually, Grace was able to compose herself, and the session continued.

"Grace, I know what you are going through, all too well. There is a very good reason why Father Williams selected me to help you cope and sort out what the rest of your life might look like. My beloved husband, Marty, died two years ago last month. And believe me, I've lived through all the things you're feeling right now. I was able to restart my life, and I can show you how that might happen for you. I can help you through the stages of grief and everything that comes with it. I think bringing us together was a wise idea on Father Williams's part. Let's prove him right."

Dr. Wall continued, "I do think Ron's death is far too tender an area to discuss at this time. Instead of speaking about the past, let's talk about the near and long term in your life. How do you see yourself and your life six months from now and a year from now? What do you see yourself doing, Grace?"

Grace thought about that for a while before answering. "Well, I sure hope that I'll have straightened out all the problems with bureaucracies and all the paperwork. But I have no idea how I'll feel about myself and about the world. I'll have to see. Will the bureaucrats succeed in giving me perforated ulcers in triplicate? Time will tell."

CHAPTER 18

A PLAN AND A JOURNEY

Grace turned to the issue foremost in her mind. "I know that Father Williams is too discreet to have filled you in on my unusual experience, but I'm sure that's what prompted his reaching out to you to set up an appointment. Ron has come to me in a dream. And I've had visits from a woman—an angel, really—who calls herself Angela. She's a psychic medium. And I don't want to get into what this all means right now, but part of me does see these visits as validation for what I promised myself, Ron, and my children.

"I told them I plan to continue Ron's work by completing his writings. Most people have old photos, cards to remember birthdays and Valentine's Day. Some have old home movies or videos to remember the good times. I have all those things, but I also have all of Ron's writings, published and unpublished. And they say so much more, with much more intimacy for me, because I was so much a part of his writing.

"I want to honor our incredible love by bringing some of Ron's story ideas to fruition. I've proofed and edited and helped on all of Ron's books, so I know his style; but I do want to add some of my own. I don't know how Ron's readers will feel about these new books, but I think writing those books with Ron as my muse, so to speak, will definitely help me. It's one more way to feel like I'm still connected to Ron.

"To be honest, I have no idea if Ron's longtime publishers will go along with this. But I will write them, and if the publishers don't want to publish them, I can always self-publish and see what happens," she said with a sense of triumph.

Dr. Wall nodded enthusiastically. "Grace, that is a fantastic idea, really fantastic. And it is such a positive thing to do. You are already inspired, and I think you'll be a wonderful writer. I really do. I'm already so happy for you."

"Thank you, Judith. But that is in the future. Today, I'm still in 'the dark days of sunshine lost,' to quote Ron. I was thinking about joining a support group for people who are severely depressed. They meet on Sunday mornings and call themselves Meet Depressed."

Dr. Wall chuckled and said, "Grace, you're so much stronger than you can begin to imagine. And while grief and depression are two sides of the same coin, we want to focus on moving past the right thing. Remember, Grace, I saw you speak at Ron's funeral. You were stunning, just incredible. I admire you.

"Two years ago, I couldn't speak at my own husband's funeral, and I don't know why. But somehow, in seeing you and hearing you speak so strongly, eloquently, and lovingly through so much intense pain, I felt you spoke for me too. And that lifted a great burden off my shoulders. I'm so very grateful to you, Grace. You helped me before I even began to help you."

Grace responded just like you would expect: with grace.

"Judith, I have no idea how I got through that eulogy for Ron. I don't even know where those words came from or how I was able to speak them. Maybe Ron wrote them, maybe love did, or maybe God did. To quote William Cowper, 'The Lord moves in mysterious ways, his wonders to perform.' I'll just say that love inspired me somehow, or maybe the horrible loss of love inspired me. I don't know. I'm just glad I made it through in a way that honored Ron and may have inspired others."

Dr. Wall said, "Well, you certainly inspired me, your family, and

I'm sure many, many others. So I have a favor to ask you. Is it okay if I become the president of your fan club?"

Grace laughed. "Your great gifts are much better served in other, more universally beneficial and therapeutic pursuits. But thank you, Judith, nevertheless."

Cue the music to the "Mutual Admiration Society" song.

"Okay, Grace, I have to get back to being Dr. Wall and not the president of your fan club. So, let's return to the subject that brings us here today: the 'dark days of sunshine lost.' How do you cope from day to day?"

Grace shrugged. "I haven't had much time to cope. I don't think I've really begun. I had a doctor's appointment one week ago. That same morning, Ron went out in a torrential rainstorm looking for my cat, Moonbeam. On Wednesday, I was told that he was dead. Thursday, our kids came back home. The wake was on Friday, the funeral was on Saturday, and last Tuesday, in the early morning, Melody and Ryder flew back to LA and back to college. This past week has been a blur. Now today is Tuesday again, and I have a doctor's appointment again. I can barely grasp what day of the week it is, much less how to cope.

"When your loved one dies, there is structure, an orderly process for what you must do. There is a wake, then a funeral, a eulogy. Easy enough to follow along. And then everyone goes home, and you are left alone. Then what? There is no defined structure to guide you along. You are adrift in a cosmic sea of fate, to grieve and mourn. Where is the structure? What do I do next? I thought the rigamarole would be the hard part, but it turns out that it wasn't. This is.

"It's like the powers that be pronounced, 'Let there be dark,' and there was darkness, and there still is. Doctor, I feel like a blind woman walking into unknown territory with nothing but my cane, my wooden eyes, to guide me. I can't see what's coming next. I'm too tired to rest and I'm too sleepy to sleep. Where does that leave me? Hell if I know.

"Ron used to say that as we get older, we become more of our authentic selves. 'We tend to move toward our destiny, to evolve or devolve into who we truly are, whether we want to or not.' It seems that now is the time when I should be discovering who I am and who I am not. Can I handle all the demands on me? I don't even know the right questions to ask. I feel like I'm looking for one needle in a haystack full of needles.

"I think about what happened with Ron, and I keep trying to make sense of this, but I feel that I'm just chasing the tail of logic. I can't find any answers that make sense to me. Right now, I only know that I have more past than future, more yesterdays than tomorrows, and more memories than hope. I'm just not the same person I used to be. So should I be trying to figure out who I am now, or am I trying to get back to that person? Where am I going? I don't know. It's hard to go on living when everything inside you has died.

"What do you do when love hurts more than it soothes and reassures? The more I loved Ron, the more it hurts. And it hurts so much more because I never got to say goodbye. I can't even form the words to tell you how painful it is to refer to Ron as my late husband, refer to him in the past tense.

"Right now, I feel like I'm standing inside the top of the hourglass, trying to find a way out. All the while, I'm thinking about the foundation of sand beneath my feet, constantly draining out from under me, into a tiny hole. And I wonder how much time I have left and what will happen next. My thoughts are random and disjointed. I don't even know if I'm making sense to you. I sound kinda nuts to myself. But thinking about a Pink Floyd song, I feel *comfortably* nuts right now."

Dr. Wall smiled, and Grace broke briefly into a full laugh, shaking her head.

"Remember, Grace, grief doesn't really come in discrete stages. It isn't just a process; it's also a journey. And you've just started this journey. You have a long way to go, with some stops along the way. I should know: I am still on my own journey. But we can't travel together.

We're on different paths with our individual timetables. That's just the way it is. And much as we may want to, you and I can't change it."

Grace sighed. "I know that, Judith. I just feel like I'm blind in three dimensions: left and right, up and down, and forward and backward. I'm just treading water in the coping department. Maybe I should linger here until I'm more certain of where I should be going. Because right now, I just want to hold on to Ron a while longer.

"I can't stop thinking how incredibly wonderful we were together. I have so many great memories and so many great questions. I don't just think about Ron and me. I think about love itself—about what love is and what it isn't. How and when does love become 'in love'? How does 'in love' become incredible love? How can love make you feel the very, very best but also make you feel the very worst, the most excruciating pain imaginable? For me, love is euphoric insanity. It's so tragic that I've lost my true love to a drainpipe, where he was searching for my beloved cat, who wasn't actually missing after all. God, please save us all from the choices we make."

Grace paused. "You know, as incredible as we were together, I can remember one Valentine's Day that wasn't very pleasant. We got into some stupid argument about I don't remember what, but the impact of that argument carried over into what Ron got me for Valentine's Day. He got me two dozen long-stemmed roses and two boxes of candies. I thought that meant everything was okay with us until I read the card that came with the roses. The card read, 'My love is like a rose; she has thorns.' And that was all it said.

"And that was all it needed to say. I knew I had a lot of hard, honest thinking to do. Neither of us said anything, but somehow it was understood that the feeling was past and would hopefully never return. And it never did. Thank you, Jesus!

"You know, Judith, as I told you, I had a visit from a psychic medium. She explained to me the reason and the circumstances of Ron's death. I was stunned to hear what she had to say. My dear friend Sally was there at the time and can confirm everything I'm telling you."

Dr. Wall's answer was succinct. "Grace, I believe you. In fact, I know she was telling the truth."

Astounded, Grace said, "How could you possibly know?"

"Angela came to me when Marty died. She was indispensable in helping me through that terrible time. So, yes, Grace, I know what you're saying, and I know that it's true because it happened to me. However, my husband didn't die for as noble a reason as Ron did—and it was noble, even if you think it was a waste. My husband died in a car crash while I was at work. Like you, I didn't have a chance to say goodbye . And I didn't know that our last kiss truly was our last kiss. So, when I tell you that I know what you are going through, Grace, I really do."

Grace spontaneously rose and leaned over to hug Judith. Now they both had loving shoulders to cry on, to cry away more and more of the endless pain.

That was enough for one day. They agreed to meet at the same time tomorrow for another session, but this time they would meet at Grace's house, in a less formal environment.

CHAPTER 19

AFTER THE VISIT

Sally saw Grace returning from her session with Dr. Wall and strode right over to her house. Grace was on the phone when she came in unannounced, so she kept quiet—until she realized that Grace was leaving her a message, asking her to come over.

Once Grace hung up, Sally declared, "I got your message and came right over."

Grace jumped, and it took her half a tick to realize that Sally had walked in on her mid-message. They both burst into cackles. That was a good start to the day for two old friends.

Sally began, "So, how did it go with Dr. Wall?"

"It was honestly wonderful, Sally, very helpful. I started out a little stiffly, but I could practically feel myself healing as we spoke. She told me that she lost her husband two years ago in a car crash. And she never had a chance to say goodbye, same as me and Ron. And, Sally, the weirdest thing of all was that Angela came to see her after her husband died too. Isn't that amazing?"

Sally suddenly looked very serious, almost nervous. "Grace, I have something important to tell you. Something I've never told another soul. You must swear to never repeat it to anyone, okay?"

Grace moved a little closer and took Sally's hand. "I will never tell another soul. I promise."

"I have to confess that I also had a visit from Angela. She came to see me when Owen died. She is some kind of messenger from God, I think. And it really is quite amazing that when we needed help the most, she was there for all three of us. When she came over to see you after Ron died, I felt I shouldn't say anything about knowing her. She was there for you, not me. I didn't want to ruin the experience for you, and I feel that I did the right thing in saying nothing. I don't want you to say anything about this to Dr. Wall, okay?"

Grace agreed, "Sally, I swear I won't say a word. Now, let's relax in front of the TV with our coffee and bagels, okay?"

As before, they eventually fell asleep on the couch and woke up with their backs hurting. It was probably time to replace the couch with something that didn't so closely resemble a medieval torture device. Sally went home, telling Grace she would come by the next day after Dr. Wall left.

Grace went to lie down and swiftly fell asleep. As she had hoped, Ron came to her once again.

"Grace, wake up, my love. It's Ron. I've come to be with you again."

This time, Grace did not waste time wondering how this could be happening. "Ron, is that you? I need you so much. Please hold me."

"I'm right here, my love. I'm here to help you as much as I can. I can't touch you, Grace, nor can you touch me, but I will help you and guide you. You should continue to see Dr. Wall. She can help you. Open up to her, my love; let her in. Be assured that you are doing the right things in the right way. She will ask you to help others going through the same thing. That is your purpose. You must help them find the true path that you are already on. They need you to inform them, inspire them, and guide them."

Through her sleepy haze, Grace said, "I understand, my love. I will try to do what you have requested of me. I just don't know if I'm ready. Oh, Ron. I still need you."

Ron lovingly replied, "Grace, my love, you are the only one who can lead them to the true path. Using all I have put you through, you must be their ladder out of the abyss, their light bulb in the darkness, their guide through the doorway to restarting their lives. Judith can't do it, Sally can't do it, and Angela can't do it. Only you can do it, my love."

Ron continued, "You have God's work to do where you are, to help these suffering people. They will continue to need your inspiration and strength, your leadership. And they will need your help and understanding when they falter. That is the unique gift only you can give them, my love—in person and through your books. Our books. That is the work God has chosen for you to do. And you must perform all this in his name. God is calling upon you, Grace. Will you do as God asks?"

"Yes, Ron, with God to strengthen me, I will do all I can."

"That is good, my love. We all serve God in our separate ways. That is our mission in life. And helping others will also help you, in much the same way that you and Judith are helping each other.

"I will continue to watch over you. Though we cannot touch physically, in spirit I will continue to kiss the top of your hand and rub it over my heart three times so that you can feel my love for you flowing from my heart and into yours. Our love transcends death and goes on forever as I await you, until that time we can truly be in each other's arms again. Till next we meet. Return to sleep and dream sweet dreams. My dreams will be of you, my love."

Grace returned fully to the escape of restful sleep.

Wednesday morning, Grace awoke refreshed. She had just enough time to eat a quick breakfast, shower, get dressed, and prepare herself and her home for the session with Dr. Wall. Judith arrived right on time. Grace greeted her at the door with a hug. They settled on the couch and drank coffee and took a moment to relax before the session officially began.

Grace started, "I already know what you're going to ask me to do,

Judith. And the answer is yes. I would be happy to."

Judith was confused. "Grace, honey, what are you talking about? What do you think I was going to ask you to do?"

"You're going to ask me to speak to your bereavement group. You want me to help them get on the true path. You want me to reach them and inspire them and maybe help them out of the darkness. You want me to be their ladder out of depression and despair, their light bulb in the darkness, guiding them to the doorway out of their misery so they can leave much of the pain behind and restart their lives. In doing so, that will somehow help you and me and them.

"Was that what you were going to ask me to do, Judith?"

Dr. Wall was astonished. "How could you possibly know that? I didn't speak to anyone about my thoughts on that matter—no one."

Grace replied simply, "Ron told me, in a dream. That's how I know. This is the work that God has asked me to do. In helping them, I am doing God's work. So I'm only too happy to help."

Dr. Wall had trouble adjusting to this revelation. "You're telling me that Ron came to you in a dream and told you this? I don't understand."

Grace was a little surprised at the doctor's surprise. She abruptly realized that although they had much in common in their experiences with Angela, her experiences with Ron were unique. So she replied, "Well, what is your scientific explanation for my knowing?"

"I don't have a scientific explanation for this. I have no explanation of any kind."

"Then just accept it, Judith. The lord moves in mysterious ways. After all, how did Angela know to come see you, or see any of us? Do you think it's because she reads the obituary notices, or is there a higher reason, a higher purpose? Just accept it, Judith. Learn to be an accepter. That's what Angela told me. It helps all of us heal."

Grace then cleared her throat to add a caveat to her statement about speaking at Judith's bereavement group. "However, there is a problem with regard to timeline. I want and need to speak to the bereavement group, especially since it is the work God has chosen for me. Yet I feel that I am not as qualified for this task as some consider me to be. I don't think I'm ready.

"I have not had the time and the focus to go through the stages of grief myself. The people in the bereavement group are likely much further along than I am. I lack credibility. I think they would be right not to accept me yet. Besides doing it so they know that I'm qualified, I have to go through the stages to benefit my own life, my own soul. So I cannot speak with the group this week. I must go through my mourning period and heal a little first; surely you understand."

Dr. Wall replied, "Grace, believe me, I know that wanting to get through the grieving process is valid and necessary, even unavoidable. But nothing messes with the process more than envisioning a deadline—in this case, a point at which you will be ready to use your experience to help others. As you know, grieving is a journey, not a goal to be surpassed. And I think you already have the ability and the intensity of spirit to get through to these suffering people and lift them up.

"I have not been able to do all that they need, Grace. You have that gift. I do not. Hopefully, working together, we can give them the means to give themselves permission to climb out of this well of despair and get back to a more productive, less painful life."

"Dr. Wall," Grace replied in measured tones, "I know how dedicated you are to helping everyone in the group. But I need to heal too. I need to go through the process the same as everyone else. That takes time, and I know that I'm not ready. I'm sorry, but I have to put my immediate needs before the needs of the group right now. They have been struggling for a long time. I am just beginning.

"I promise you that I will do all I can to help the members of the group. I just cannot do that without beginning the work myself. Look, I already feel selfish about this, but I need me right now more than they need me. That is my decision."

Dr. Wall's smile was a little sad. "I see that I've gone from Judith to Dr. Wall to you, and I accept that. I also accept your decision to wait to speak to the group until a later time. I hope that doesn't mean an end to our friendship. And while I've been, shall I say, overly enthusiastic in my expectation of all you could do to help the group with your unique gifts, your strength, and your skills, my first responsibility to you is my professional responsibility as your psychiatrist."

Dr. Wall added, "I hope my eagerness to involve you in the group hasn't damaged our professional relationship either. I do hope you will continue to meet with me. I will help you with your journey through the process and answer any questions. When you feel that the time is right for you, please call me, and we can set up another appointment and see how it goes."

Grace nodded silently, a little overwhelmed by the unexpected pressure she felt to fulfill God's purpose for her.

"Until that time, Grace, take good care of yourself, my dear friend."

After Dr. Wall left, Grace called Sally, asking her to visit. Worried by Grace's urgency, her friend came right over.

"So, I just spoke with Dr. Wall," Grace began as they settled at her kitchen table. "I told her that Ron visited me again in my sleep. He told me that Dr. Wall would ask me to speak to her bereavement group. When I told her what Ron told me, she was flabbergasted. How could I possibly know? She felt that since I spoke so well at the funeral, I could make a similar speech to her group. I told her that I could not do that at this time. I don't feel qualified to speak to a group of people who have been mourning for a long time when I myself have not had the time to process that my other half is gone. So, Sally, my beloved best friend, I need your help yet again.

"Just so you know, I've almost taken care of the innumerable problems with the insurance company, etc.—all the bureaucracies. I've even handled the kid's tuition needs and set up separate accounts for them. But there is a lot more I need to take care of within me. I really need you to understand this and help my family and friends to understand this as well."

Sally answered, "I will do whatever you need, Grace. Just tell me what that is."

"I need to withdraw into a deeper level of solitude. I need time to work on me. I need to turn inward to move forward; to more purposefully simplify my life; to solve problems that are mine and mine alone, whether they are real or imagined; to try to solve my mental, emotional, interpersonal issues on my own, for myself, by myself. I need to see for myself a path out of this quagmire, this morass of grief, depression, and pulverizing powerlessness. Perhaps grief is like a fog, or smoke, which slowly dissipates. Or maybe it's like driving through a thick cloud up to a high mountain peak: you eventually get to the top and see daylight again. I hope to discover the truth about that as I surrender myself fully to the sorrow threatening to consume me. I must let it consume me. And all that, I must do alone.

"Sally, I need to greatly reduce communication with the outside world, including my children, my family, even with you, my beloved, amazing best friend. I need to fully and completely mourn Ron, without distraction. Furthermore, I need you to be my castle walls and my shield, to protect me in this vulnerable time. Like a telephone, I'm forwarding my life to your life, for you to let everyone know that I'm okay. I just need to isolate myself from everyone for a while. This is a sacrifice I need from them and from you too.

"I mean, I will see you here and there. I still have to go out to get groceries and cat food and such, but then I will return to the private, mournful solitude here in my hermitage. We'll still wave to each other through the kitchen window or see each other once in a while for lunch or something. You'll know that I am okay. And you can communicate that to all the others.

"To take care of all the people I love, including you, I must follow my own timetable. I'm sure you understand."

Sally took Grace's hand. "Grace, my beloved friend, I love you deeply and will do all you ask and need. I will always be here for you. I will see you at the other end of the tunnel, or sooner if you need me. Just remember to love yourself as much as everyone else loves you."

CHAPTER 20

THE REAL GRIEVING BEGINS

When Sally left, Grace was genuinely alone—except, of course, for her devoted four-legged psychiatrist, Dr. Moonbeam, to whom she could tell all her secrets and troubles. She went upstairs to her extra-large, extra-lonely king-sized bed. Shortly thereafter, she had a house call from Dr. Moonbeam, the master cuddler, who had a wonderful bedside manner. Grace imagined she heard her say, "Just lie down and tell me all about it."

They both fell asleep almost immediately and slept for hours. A healing sleep was such a wonderful escape from her torment and despair. And with sleep, not only are all things possible, but they're actually quite likely.

When Grace awoke, it was late afternoon, early evening. The sun was low in the west. She remembered a poem Ron had written for her years ago when they were on the beach at Big Sur, right around sunset.

She repeated one line out loud: "The last light of sun so brightly ablaze, in a yellow, orange and reddish haze, says to me that this day is done, as the west eats up and swallows the sun."

Moonbeam seemed to like Ron's poem, looking up briefly and nuzzling closer to her mommy's robe, where she purred and purred. Grace watched the news for a while, petting Moonbeam, who had her mommy all to herself now. She headed downstairs just before the commercials came on. A wise choice. It was time to prepare dinner—first for Her Majesty, Queen Moonbeam, of course, and then later on for herself. She ate her dinner in front of the TV. Having eaten her dinner, Moonbeam curled back up in mommy's soft, thick robe for a long cuddle.

During an endless commercial break, Grace considered what to do with all her free time and solitude. She could finally watch all those DVDs they'd bought but never found the time for. She could watch the complete series of *The Twilight Zone* and *MacGyver* and many more. She and Ron had loved to watch those shows together. Now watching those shows would remind her of the wonderful times they'd spent cuddling. *And he will be right there with me again.*

With that thought, Grace broke into sobs welling from a place deeper within herself than she'd ever delved. The grief process was well underway.

Sensing her feelings, Doc Moonbeam crawled up to reassure her, licking her face and breaking Grace's crying cycle long enough to appreciate Moonbeam's steadfast support, love, and dedication. Petting the furry creature from head to tail, Grace decided that Dr. Moonbeam was a wonderful doctor. *She certainly relieved my pain and made me feel a helluva lot better, just like a real doctor should.*

Scanning the channels on cable, Grace found a delightful old movie from 1963, in glorious black and white. The film was *A Child Is Waiting*, starring Burt Lancaster and Judy Garland in a dramatic role. Unfortunately, in the emptiness of her bedroom, the sound seemed to bounce off the walls, reminding her that it was empty because Ron was not there, amplifying the loneliness of her solitude.

In the film, Judy Garland plays a music teacher at a state institution, teaching music to mentally disabled and emotionally disturbed children. *I'm a former music teacher watching a movie about a music teacher. I like the poetry of this*, Grace thought.

When the movie was over, it was time for bed. Moonbeam was happy and content, so neither moved. As Grace lay back in her bed, she felt more alone this night than she had felt last night. She had cut herself off from her best friend and her family. It was time to begin paying the heavy price for having loved so hard. Well, as Lao Tzu wrote, "A journey of a thousand miles begins with a single step."

Grace let herself lapse into a reverie shared only with Ron, though she didn't see him as she did when she was asleep.

"You know, Ron, our home has always been our Fortress of Solitude, our comfort, our retreat. Now, without you, this house has become a vast cavern, empty and lonely. Maybe this house is haunting me. All the great memories, past laughter, birthdays, Christmases, and all the other holidays with all the kids and other family—they all shout at me.

"I cannot even find pleasure in any of my music. And I need that escape. But I am so conscious of listening to it all alone, without you, my love. I have lost the two most reliable sources of comfort and security in my life, lost to the thundering isolation of your not being here with me."

Hopefully Ron will be the dream that comes to me. Grace had fallen into the habit and the expectation of having contact with Ron every night. She felt like a child on Christmas Eve, willing herself to sleep in expectation of a very special visitor. Only sleep would reveal whether he came. Yet Grace remained wide awake. *Dammit, what a rotten night to have insomnia. Will Ron feel rejected because I can't get to sleep right away?*

Perhaps she could take a sleeping pill. But why risk falling into a dreamless sleep? She decided to play nature sounds on her clock radio—waves crashing on the shoreline, rainfall. *But maybe that will make me have to pee all night long.*

Too late; she had finally fallen asleep, much to the relief of Moonbeam.

∼

Grace woke up Thursday morning with a heavy pressure on her heart. Ready to call 911, she immediately realized it was Moonbeam sitting on her chest, jabbing her jaw with a soft paw. Worse than the "almost" heart attack early in the morning, she couldn't remember Ron coming to her in the night. *Bummer!*

Well, the furry alarm clock had made the command decision that it was time for Her Majesty to have her breakfast. Speaking in the royal we, the queen of the house clearly stated, "We are not amused! Where is our breakfast?" It was past time for Grace to get to work.

When the most critical part of her morning was completed, Grace was granted permission to prepare something for her own breakfast.

She made it easy for herself this morning, just coffee and cereal. She brought everything into the living room to watch the tube for breakfast; it was the standard morning news with the standard talking heads telling everyone what great shape the world was in. The media's "common-taters"—or "average spuds," as Ron called them—were pontificating as always. The world was in such terrible shape that the only thing that could save it was *more commercials*!

Grace had had enough. She found a channel playing *The Little Rascals*. Finally, a constructive use for her TV. Something uplifting at last!

When *The Little Rascals* ended, Grace got another cup of coffee. She decided it was time for a step-by-step review of the stages of grief. She wanted to see where she was on the list, but that was difficult to assess as she scanned over the printout. She might feel one way, but Sally, her children, Dr. Wall, and Father Jerry might have very different perspectives on where she was and what she should be doing. And they all loved her.

Well, Grace thought, *I've read the info; I'll think about it throughout the day and see how I feel later.*

She contemplated going outside to check the mail. But she did not look forward to the mail. So much of it was not for her. Ron was still getting bills, adding to the list of things she thought she'd completed. And she didn't know what to do with letters from readers. She felt she owed it to them to write individual letters. After all, she wanted them to be her readers when she finished Ron's books. But she was not ready to do that yet. *Soon, but not yet*, she told herself.

Grace's next crisis was well underway: in her hermitage, in her manufactured solitude, she was already bored to death. What to do next, if anything? She ended up lying in bed, completely awake, trying to sell herself on going back to sleep.

After a while, she got up and closed her bedroom drapes. That might have helped Moonbeam sleep, but Grace realized there was too much for her to do—or not to do. She decided to play solitaire on her computer since she was already in solitary confinement, by her own choosing. Of course, her boredom followed her to the computer to keep her company. Maybe Dr. Moonbeam had some ideas. Unfortunately, Moonbeam was successfully asleep with her Do Not Disturb sign written across her belly. Grace would have to think of something else.

She wondered, *Is total boredom part of the grieving process? Or have I even started the actual grieving process? How am I to know?* On her second official day of grieving in her self-manufactured exile, she felt she should be thinking about Ron all the time, but she wasn't. *Maybe I'm too focused on doing things right to just do it. Or maybe this is what really happens to people when they lose someone, but they don't talk about it.*

"I don't know," she said aloud. "It seems too early to check in with Dr. Wall. Maybe I'll go over to see Sally?" But it also seemed too early to see Sally. Grace had just told her yesterday that she wouldn't be seeing her or anyone else for a while.

Grace went into the kitchen, hoping to at least spot Sally through her window and give her a wave. Sally was nowhere to be seen, though her car was parked outside, so Grace knew she was home. She argued herself out of marching over. *If I call or knock on her door,*

I might wake her up. With all the stress she's been through, she needs her sleep as much as I do. What's wrong with me? I should be able to figure all this out. She couldn't help waffling between calling Sally or calling Dr. Wall. Unsure what to do, she went back to bed. It almost seemed to her to be a form of pacing; instead of walking around, she was hopping on and off the bed.

Lying there, she finally got an idea. She went downstairs to look through all the old family photo albums. Maybe that would spark something in her and move her along in the grieving process, like thinking about the movies and shows they used to watch had done.

She saw the very first ever photos of the kids, in the maternity ward, right after they were both born. And there was Ron, the proud daddy. She didn't feel mournful seeing Ron there. She just felt grateful to God and so happy and proud. That was the first photo of her new family. She and Ron were overjoyed as the newborns yawned from boredom or tiredness, or both.

She pored through more family photos. The more she saw, the happier and prouder she became. A few minutes later, Grace was asleep with the photos in her lap. Looking at the family photos had been just the hug she needed.

Grace woke up a few hours later to an impatient, neglected Moonbeam, whose dinner was quite late. Moonbeam had that "We are not amused" look on her mug. Grace might end up on "official probation" for such a severe disregard of the house rules!

Once properly admonished, her profuse apologies given, Grace was allowed to get on with her most urgent, most sacred mission: preparing dinner for Queen Moonbeam. Later on, she was allowed to prepare a light repast for herself. Grace glanced up from the kitchen to see Sally waving at her. Sally gave her a thumbs-up and a smile. Grace responded in kind, her mouth almost hurting from her huge smile. Happy and reassured that all was okay and life goes on, the friends went back to their individual tasks.

Grace decided to get some fresh bagels in the morning and invite herself to Sally's. A day had passed, the longest she'd gone without speaking to her good friend in years.

Now with a plan and a path forward, Grace found a reason for optimism.

CHAPTER 21

FRESH BAGELS WITH SALLY

Grace was up first thing in the morning and stalled by making pancakes so that she didn't get to Sally's house too early.

Blueberry pancakes had been the last meal Ron had prepared for her on that fateful day and the breakfast she had cooked for her family after Ron died. Sooner or later, she would most likely get into that "Why cook for just one person" rut and just microwave something for herself in the mornings.

She sat down to a leisurely breakfast in front of the TV, as people who live alone frequently do, but elected not to watch the news since she wanted to keep her breakfast down. She found an old *Twilight Zone* rerun: "Time Enough at Last," starring Burgess Meredith. Somehow, his character survives World War III inside a bank vault. Now, with the city flattened and everyone gone, except for the library, there is finally plenty of time to read his beloved books. And Grace had time enough to grieve; how poignant.

After the show, she cleaned the dishes and checked the clock. She had wasted enough time to shower, get "fresh out of the oven" bagels, and head over to Sally's without worrying about waking her friend up.

Grace just wanted bagels. Some of the other customers just wanted to talk about Ron dying in a drainpipe. She found it extra challenging to indulge the ghouls. Luckily, the bakery's owner, Ben, read the situation and got her out of there quickly so that she could leave the disappointed gossips behind.

As she drove back home, she wondered, *Is this what I must endure every time I go shopping for groceries and everything else? Maybe I can just order what I need on the computer or the phone and have it delivered.* That sounded like a more workable solution for avoiding inquiring minds.

Once Grace was home and settled and more relaxed after her unexpected rush of irritation at the bakery, she called Sally.

"Hi, Sally, it's your long-lost neighbor. I know it's been an incredibly long time since we spoke—when I told you that I was going to join the Foreign Legion and wouldn't see you for a while. Well, I got back this morning, and I got some fresh-baked bagels from Ben's Bakery. I thought you might enjoy some. Would you enjoy them more at your house or my house?"

Sally answered, "Well, that depends on who makes the better coffee, me or you. I just pushed a button to make some, but you'll have to get it while it's hot. You've got two minutes to get over here, or it will be burnt."

"Goodness," Grace said. "You're putting me under a lot of pressure. Luckily, I already have my running shoes on. They should make all the difference. Be there in half a tick, and not a tock more."

Grace grabbed the bag of bagels and some strawberry-flavored cream cheese and made the mad dash over to Sally's.

"You're too late. The coffee is burnt," Sally greeted her.

Grace retorted, "That's okay, Sally, the bagels are three days past their expiration date."

"Great," Sally responded. "Let's eat."

They sat in Sally's kitchen and immediately began fighting over who got which bagel. Of course, as they shared the Wisdom of Solomon, both of the bagels they wanted were split in two; Solomon would be pleased. They talked about anything and everything, as long as the subject didn't touch on Grace ending her seclusion.

Finally, Grace addressed the elephant: "Sally, I have thoroughly read and re-read the information I have on the seven stages of grief, so I understand what to expect logically. They seem straightforward, but I don't feel confident that I know how to get from one stage to another. There appears to be no clear pathway for me to follow. I'm stuck.

"I've tried sleeping a lot. That hasn't worked. I've tried looking at old photo albums to see if that would trigger a significant response. I don't know if I'm ready to look at old photos and videos of our wedding. That might make me too depressed. But then, maybe not. Looking at family photos just filled me with joy.

"In simple terms, I'm ashamed to tell you that I am bored to death. That suggests to me that I must be doing something wrong. I should be feeling terribly, terribly sad, inconsolable. But I haven't gotten to that place yet, and I don't know how or if it's nuts to want to get there.

"I'm not even sure where I am in the stages. I may be further behind than I think I am, or further ahead. I know that I have the time and the solitude I thought were necessary conditions to go through this process, but I am missing something, and I don't know what that piece is. I do have a theory, though. I think it is because Ron did not come to me in my dreams these last two nights—to tell me what to do, to guide me, to reassure me and love me. And since you've been through everything, Sally, I've come to you for your advice and wisdom. What am I doing wrong? What should I be doing?"

Sally had been expecting this, in one form or another, but suddenly felt pressured to think of something profound to say.

Finally, the Voice of all Wisdom spoke: "Grace, Grace, Grace. From my perspective, the conditions you have created are right, and you're doing everything correctly. It's just that the process is *nuts*! Because it's different for every individual, as you know.

"The process I went through was right for me, but it wouldn't necessarily be right for you, and I don't know that I can even describe or define it. My deeply loved friend, you must trust your pathway.

And trust in time. I believe in its healing power. It healed me, and I think it will heal you too. But time takes time. So give it that time. Continue as you have been doing. And see how things go.

"We can talk whenever you think we should. And maybe you should see Dr. Wall again, if that feels right. It would be wise to get a second opinion. I do have a suggestion for you, though: Consider going through Ron's uncompleted story ideas. See if going through his writings might open up some doors for you. After all, you said you planned on finishing some of his drafts and ideas. Maybe now is the time to begin."

Grace was a tad astonished at the simplicity and rightness of Sally's suggestion and nodded vigorously. *Why didn't I think of that?*

Sally continued, "Now, for that advice, I charge two bagels and a second cup of coffee. Are we going to fight over the last blueberry bagel, or will you let me have it?"

Grace answered, "I pay my bills, Sally, especially for house calls. It's all yours."

∼

When Grace got home, she went downstairs to Ron's den, over to his desk where he wrote—his "lonely writer's garret," his "exploratoreum," as he called it. To the right stood two file cabinets and a bookshelf. One file cabinet and the bookshelf contained his completed manuscripts and books, respectively. The other file cabinet was for his uncompleted writing projects and story ideas and such. She spent a little time reminiscing over some of his completed works. Every book, every manuscript, brought back many pleasant memories. She smiled at Ron's achievements. Grace had seen these stories grow from their embryonic forms all the way to their completed states; she had been a big part of their creation—always the first to read them and offer her advice and editing skills—and often helped Ron decide on their endings.

Ron gave Grace lavish praise in his books for her enormous contribution to his work. She was his muse, his inspiration. That thought made her smile and brought her a surge of confidence in undertaking this writing project.

Grace closed the file cabinet of Ron's completed work and delved into Ron's unfinished stories and story ideas. The full wisdom of Sally's advice hit her immediately. Grace could spend a lot of time wading through Ron's files while her grief slowly simmered and evaporated in the background on a very low flame, which she could stir from time to time, as necessary.

She was definitely on the right track now. She could work on writing the stories while mourning her lost love. Perhaps in this way, Ron could somehow be her muse, her inspiration, just as she had been his. *Thank you, Sally! You are so amazingly brilliant and so very, very wise!*

She would have to go through all the papers in the file cabinet and categorize and organize them in a system that made sense to her. Well, as the old proverb goes, "There's no time like the present."

She couldn't possibly accomplish much without her music playing in the background. She put in some Judy Collins, Joan Baez, Buffy Sainte Marie, Sade, Joni Mitchell, and, of course, some Laura Nyro CDs, and began her long project. Part of her enthusiasm came from her ability to enjoy her music again.

She began labeling stacks by which to categorize the papers from the file cabinet. Luckily, Ron had already started putting things in file folders, albeit very disorganized ones.

"This is gonna take a lot of time, a lot of great music, and a lot of work!" she declared.

But Grace has plenty of time and solitude to focus on the task at hand, with great music and no distractions. Correction: one major distraction, and she was getting hungry. Her Majesty insisted on promptness!

"Yes, Moonbeam, Mommy is on her way up to feed you."

The following morning, Grace got back to her literary project. This would take much more time to figure out than she had first anticipated. She soon ran out of room on the desk. What she really needed were file boxes. Luckily, she knew where Ron put everything in his office because she was the one who organized it for him. Eventually, she emptied and sorted everything from one file cabinet into its proper boxes.

She could more fully review where she stood regarding the work to be done at her leisure. After all, she had time, purpose, and structure. For now, she gave herself permission to take a nap.

Later on, she would feed "the queen" her royal cat food and hopefully make dinner for herself. Either she'd watch TV for dinner or begin going through one of the file boxes of Ron's writings. But for right now, she went upstairs alone. Now she was the one hiding out. The cat could go looking for her for a change. *I'll show her who the mommy is.* Of course, Moonbeam found Grace before Grace found her own bed.

Grace and Moonbeam lay down for a well-deserved nap. They were both asleep in minutes. While she was deep asleep, Ron came to her.

He said, "Grace, my love, it's Ron. I've come to speak with you again. There are some very important things I have to tell you."

In her dreamy state, Grace answered, "Oh, Ron, oh, my love, I've waited so long to be with you again. It's been so very difficult not seeing you."

"I know, my love. But though you don't always see me, know that I am with you. The reason I can visit you like this today is because you took Sally's wonderful, brilliant advice and began to go through my unfinished writings in the file cabinet. By performing that step, you brought me to you."

"Ron," she said, "I'm so confused. I'm stuck. I don't know if I'm doing everything properly or not. I need your help, your guidance. What should I do next?"

"Grace, my love, there's no such thing as 'properly' with this sort of thing. Anything you're doing is right and at the right pace. You're on the right road. You just have to travel further down it. You are preparing to do God's work. But you were right to postpone speaking to Dr. Wall's bereavement group until you are better prepared to speak to them. And writing will help to ground you and focus you.

"Grace, I have to go now. I will see you again."

"Ron, I have a deep need to be with you. Can't you stay just a little longer? Ron? Ron? Are you still here?"

Grace jerked fully awake and sensed that Ron was gone. She knew there was nothing she could do right now, but it took her quite some time to get back to sleep.

That worried her. But she eventually fell into a deep sleep as Moonbeam snuggled closer, putting off the heart-to-heart talk she would have with Mommy about a very serious problem that demanded corrective attention: *Mommy steals the covers*!

CHAPTER 22

THE LONG AND WINDING ROAD

The afternoon nap turned into an all-nighter. When Grace woke up, the morning was well underway. She took extra time to stretch and then turned on "the tube" on the dresser. As always, the morning news featured the regular collection of "average spuds" droning on with their predictably banal banter, giving the media's position on the day's news. Time to switch to Animal Planet and something more uplifting than the news.

Having slept through last night's dinner for both herself and Moonbeam, Grace was starving. She and an incensed, noisy Moonbeam went down to the kitchen for breakfast. She made bacon, sausages, and eggs with toast. Whenever she made eggs, she made two so that the hardworking Moonbeam could have one with her breakfast—maybe even some sausage and bacon for an extra-hungry cat this morning. Grace took her breakfast to the living room, plopping herself back in front of the TV.

She decided to call her children to say hello and let them know that she was okay and making progress in her mourning, even if she didn't know how to describe that progress. Ryder and Melody were happy and reassured to hear that Mom was feeling well. They hadn't wanted to call her at the wrong time, so they hadn't called at all, instead waiting for Sally's updates. Grace then called Sally to say hello and share that she had taken her friend's advice and was sorting the contents of Ron's file cabinet as a first step. She planned to thoroughly review one of the boxes today. Sally encouraged her to do so.

Grace intended to write a summary of what each story was about. She would then determine which of the stories she was most capable of continuing and which one she would begin work on first. In addition, part of her wanted to see how going through this process would affect her and where it would take her emotionally.

But what she put her hand on first was a folder of notes to her. The first one read,

> How incredibly blessed we are to have found each other.
> We are two concentric circles, sharing a common center.

She thought that was charming and, of course, accurate. Her throat tickled, but the tears didn't immediately erupt. *Let me try one more for now.*

> Grace, when I hold you in my arms, my love, I hold my own beating heart.

That was it; Grace wailed and wailed. Moonbeam woke up and ran to Mommy's side to comfort her, wondering if she should call Sally or 911. But Grace's furry companion would not leave her mommy's side, where she knew she was most needed.

∼

As if sensing Grace's emotional turmoil, or perhaps expecting it after Grace's phone call the day before, Sally came over late the following morning to check on her. She couldn't find Grace, and she couldn't find Moonbeam. *Oh God, not this again!* Sally called Grace's name. No response. But Moonbeam came up from the basement, so Sally went down to look for her friend.

Grace was lying on the carpet, Ron's papers in her hands.

Somehow, Sally got her onto the sofa in the basement. Grace was quite groggy. With a great deal of effort, Sally eventually got her friend into her own bed. Grace had slept on the floor, but what quality of sleep?

Sally fed Moonbeam a big breakfast. It was likely that she had missed another meal last night.

Then Sally brought coffee and bagels for both of them to Grace's bedroom. *This should be the cure. For both of us.*

Grace strained her eyes and said, "Where are we? Who are you?"

"My name is Moonbeam; what's yours?" came Sally's quick reply.

Grace giggled, and her friend followed suit. The fog was lifting. Grace was getting back to abnormal.

Sally asked, "So, how did we get here?"

"I started reading some of the material in Ron's 'unfinished works' file cabinet," Grace explained. "Some of it was just story ideas, as you would expect. But some of it was very personal and, under these circumstances, emotionally overwhelming. I just burst into tears and couldn't stop crying. I don't know what happened after that."

"Well, Grace, grief is a long, long journey. I'm sure Dr. Wall told you that."

Grace just nodded.

"The experience you had yesterday was part of the toll. It's good for you. And I expect there will be more of these episodes to come. In fact, I encourage you to seek them out. Read more of Ron's writings, cry more tears, go further and further down that road. It will take you where you need to be."

When Sally headed home, Grace lay in bed and thought about what her friend had said and what she should do next. Going through Ron's writings had provided the most significant release for her sorrow since her children had returned to school. She craved more;

she needed more. So, she took a shower and got dressed. *Maybe I should prepare a big meal for Moonbeam right now*. She felt guilty about starving the royal terror and didn't want the distraction.

Moonbeam didn't know quite what to do with these alternating periods of feast and famine.

Now more energized, Grace headed for the basement, back to Ron's notes. The first one she read sounded like Ron was either writing to himself or trying to clarify something he wanted to say.

> *Certain memories unquestionably must and shall remain hidden away in that special place. Distant, but accessible with effort. Not locked away, just put away, to be preserved and protected. To be visited and remembered only on special occasions. Or when there is need, for comfort and reassurance, before moving on again.*

That one certainly hit close to home. It sounded like something Ron had written after his mother's death. *It feels like a message for me since I'm now in that same situation*. The next paper she found was their wedding invitation, which put a smile on her face. Ron had written something unusual and clever on the wedding invitations, a code just for the two of them: 2 2 B 1, and the date of their wedding, meaning "two to be one." *That was Ron for you*.

The next one was short:

> *Time happens all by itself, but love, love takes work, lots of work.*

That may have been written after an argument, she thought wryly.

The next one was very tender.

> *I want to feel like home to you, warm, safe, secure, and comfortable.*

"That sounds so much like Ron," Grace told Moonbeam, who

seemed only politely interested. "That's one that will make me cry and cry but will get me further down the road in my grief. And as difficult and painful as that will be for me, that's what I have to do. That's what I have to endure."

Grace continued reading Ron's notes, learning more and more about her husband and loving him even more if possible.

> With you, Grace, my heart has had to grow a little larger every day, to fit all of your love into my life. My heart has become deeper and wider and even more loving because of the purity of your love. You have filled my life to overflowing.

"Oh, Ron, that is so beautiful."

> Maybe we each see something in the other that we have been looking for separately but have found in one another.

The tears flowing down her face were happy ones.
She decided to pace herself and read just a few more.
The next one began,

> The winged mind takes flight and soars where birds can see but cannot go, the envy of eagles.

She liked that one very much. Rummaging through the box, she found a few notes inside a rubber band that seemed to be about writing. *That looks like excellent inspiration*, she thought with satisfaction.

One read,

> Writing undresses a writer, leaving him exposed, vulnerable, and naked before an unworthy world. The only fig leaf left for him is what is written. But even those words provide no modesty, leaving him bare before the molestations of loathsome critics.

> *What defense does the writer have? Perhaps silent letters will speak up for him. But alas, silent letters say nothing. They speak only to mimes. But who speaks for silent letters? Why, Harpo Marx, of course. Thank you, Harpo.*

Grace could practically hear Ron saying these words. The next one read,

> *I whisper to my pen, and it writes down what I say.*
> *And though it's there on paper, it still won't go away.*
> *It rattles in my head, too big to escape my ears.*
> *Then by some writer's alchemy, on the page it appears.*

Grace laughed, "That's my Ron."
The next one was just a snippet:

> *Giving words and a voice to a world of mumblers.*

Then:

> *The Tao of Writing, the Way of the Pen.*

Maybe just one or two more, she thought.

> *I try to find the funny in the true and the everyone in all of us.*

> *Summers are always hot. Summer hotter than others.*

That's a funny one. Ron must have been playing with words for his amusement.

Grace hadn't discovered as many pent-up tears on this go-round, but she was ready for a break nonetheless. It was time for lunch and a nap. *The Prisoner* with Patrick McGoogan would be coming on shortly, and she didn't want to miss the very best TV series ever created.

After *The Prisoner*, the ladies took a nap in Moonbeam's boudoir. Lying there, Grace marveled at Ron's excellence as a writer. *No wonder he won all those awards!* She soon fell asleep.

A few hours later, refreshed after her nap, Grace returned to reading Ron's notes.

The first one she laid her hands on read,

> Grace, your intelligence stimulates my mind almost as much as your beauty stimulates my hormones. When I behold your delicious beauty, it takes me at least an hour to get my eyes back into my head and my tongue back into my mouth.

Grace laughed. "Well, there goes the G rating. Yep, that's Ron, all right; I would know that horny little devil anywhere. Oh, sweet Jesus, I miss you so much, Ron!"

∼

Going through all the file boxes of Ron's writing was quite an undertaking. But that was okay. She grieved and healed with each passing day and each passing week. The next steps required careful thought and consideration. Ron's writings, as well as Grace's future as a writer, deserved that meticulousness.

She eventually focused on his partially completed stories to determine which had the most "Ron" in them. Then she would complete one of them with her own writing. That was her plan.

She took a break one afternoon to grab lunch for herself and her constant companion and most ardent supporter, Lady Moonbeam. As she ate at her kitchen table and read over Ron's material, she decided that one story was a definite contender. She wanted to find at least three workable manuscripts from which she would select the one she thought was the best fit for his publishers, his readers, and for herself as a writer to work on first.

The other contenders could follow, regardless of how the publishers and the public received them. After all, she was ultimately writing for herself, and for Ron. She wanted Ron Butler and Grace Butler side by side on the cover—that is, if the publishers and their lawyers allowed it.

∼

Grace continued searching for the next "winner," not quite ready to sit down and write. Her thorough review of every single piece of paper in all the boxes went on for almost two months. Finally, she had her three strong nominees. She also had the order in which she wanted to write them.

In celebration of her accomplishment, she gave herself permission to enjoy a movie. She chose *A Funny Thing Happened on the Way to the Forum* for a well-deserved good laugh. Tomorrow, she would officially begin work on the first book.

Grace had the great idea to ask Sally if she wanted to join her for the movie. Besides phone calls a few times a week and the occasional visit, they had not enjoyed each other's company for quite some time.

Sally's reply was "I'll come right over. But you'd better microwave some popcorn."

They made it about ten minutes into the movie before passing out over the arms of the sofa yet again. Luckily, Moonbeam stayed up and ate all the popcorn. Cats have never been found guilty of wasting food.

When Grace and Sally finally woke up, they were two older ladies in need of traction. They squinted at each other, then at the cat. Moonbeam had traces of popcorn in her whiskers and a "Who, me?" look on her guilty little mug.

Sally said, "Do you think she liked the movie?"

Grace snickered, "Looks like 'two paws up' to me!"

Sally suggested, "Grace, I'll buy you a new couch that won't hurt our backs if you buy me a new back."

"I've got your back on that one, Sally."

They glanced at each other again and laughed and laughed.

Neither knew the time of day, but Sally knew it was time to go home. She thanked Grace for inviting her over and remarked, "Who knows? Someday we may actually see the movie."

Sally went home while Grace and the cat headed upstairs. Lying in bed, petting Moonbeam, Grace reflected on where she was mentally. She had accomplished the goal of sorting out Ron's unfinished writings. She had thoroughly reviewed every piece of paper in the file boxes. She'd decided on the unfinished stories she would complete. And she knew the order she wanted to work on them. The only thing left to do was begin writing.

Tomorrow morning, she decided. She felt a sense of accomplishment and order in her life. She felt in control of her own life, her destiny. Now she could relax for a while and get some real rest.

Grace drifted easily into a deep sleep, opening the door for Ron to come to her.

"Grace, it's Ron. Once again you have made it possible for me to speak with you. I'm here."

Through the half-asleep, blue, misty haze, she murmured, "Thank you, merciful God, thank you. You're really here with me now, Ron. It's been weeks. I have so much to tell you."

"Yes, Grace. You did exactly what you said you would. You went through my unfinished projects, and you selected the stories you want to complete. And you made three wonderful choices."

"Thank you, Ron. That is what I wanted to tell you, my beloved."

Ron answered, "Yes, Grace, my love. I watch over you as best I can. I am so very proud of you. You're amazing! I love you more and more. And there is something else you should know, Grace. There are others here who are watching over you and know all you do as well. It is because you have followed through on what you said you would do; you have begun the process to complete my books. By doing so, you have made it possible for me to speak with you today. They are so pleased with you and wish me to help and guide you in completing these stories."

"Ron," she whispered, "I'm overwhelmed with everything that happened and how it happened. Thank God, and thank you too, Ron. I feel that such a tremendous burden has been lifted off my shoulders now. I feel uplifted and optimistic, like everything is possible. My path is clear. I will do my very best to honor your work in my writing, my love. This is surely the triumph of love over death."

Ron's answer was brief. "As you write, you will feel my presence. I have to go now. Good night, my beloved."

She slept with a smile and was still smiling when she awoke the following morning. She wasn't sure what portion of her journey she had passed through last night, but she was convinced she had passed through something. Perhaps a tunnel, perhaps a door—definitely something important.

Things were different now. She didn't have the full picture of how everything had changed, but she was confident all would become clear in time. *Who knows, maybe I completed one of the stages?* Whatever it was, she was happy she had a positive update for Sally.

Grace called her friend to invite herself over for breakfast. Sally replied, "Hello, lucky. You must be psychic or something. I just got back home a few minutes ago from Ben's Bakery. I got some fresh bagels for us. I was planning to come over for breakfast, but you called me before I could call you, so now you have to make the trek."

When Grace arrived, the negotiations began.

"First things first: I get the blueberry bagel. House rules!"

Grace answered, "As long as I get cinnamon raisin. Agreed?"

They both faked spitting on their hands and shook on it. A done deal.

Grace began, "Sally, dear, as you know, I have been going through Ron's writings. I've selected three strong stories that Ron began, and

I will pick up where he left off and complete the writing of these books. That's the first part of what I wanted to tell you. The other part is that Ron came to me in my sleep last night. He is aware of everything I've done, and he is very pleased. So pleased, Sally, that he will help me and guide my writing by telling me how he planned to write the rest of the story. Isn't that great, Sally?"

Sally took a moment to consider what she would say next, knowing it would be important. She began, "Grace, my dear friend. I'm thrilled you took my advice and started doing just what you said you would. But consider this: if Ron is helping you to write, does that make him a 'ghostwriter'?"

Body-shaking belly laughs overtook them—the type that make you cry from laughter.

When their laughter subsided sometime later, Sally's face became serious as she studied her friend. This made Grace nervous.

"Grace, something has happened to you. You're different in some way. I'm not quite sure how, but you're not the Grace who gave that incredible eulogy at Ron's funeral. You are an evolved, accomplished Grace, and I am so happy for you and so very proud. I truly feel graced by your friendship and your love."

Grace didn't know what to say after such a huge compliment. She spilled grateful tears and gave big, long hugs. What a great report card from her teacher.

"You're right, as always. I feel that somehow I've passed through something, and I'm on the other side."

Sally studied Grace again, noting the relaxed muscles of her face, the easy smile that didn't seem to leave her lips, and the sparkle in her eyes.

"I think I know what it is, Grace. I think that by some miracle, you have reached a point past the seven stages of grief far sooner than most others. Maybe, somehow, you were transported through a sort of grief 'wormhole.' I know the stages are very subjective, and I don't know how you were able to do it, but I think you did.

"Maybe it's just an incredible gift bestowed on you because of the incredible, veil-crossing love you and Ron share. I think it may be that you are being prepared for something extraordinary, something significant. Of course, it's just a guess. And as for passing through most or all of the stages, part of the reason is perhaps that you haven't really lost your spouse forever, as I and Dr. Wall and so many others have. You spoke together just last night. I'm not sure I envy you. I don't know how I would handle hearing and seeing Owen and being unable to touch him. But maybe that is how all this was made possible for you.

"You have a destiny to fulfill, girlfriend. Go off and meet it. Go see Dr. Wall and tell her everything you told me, as well as everything I told you."

CHAPTER 23

REUNITING WITH DR. WALL

When Grace got home, she immediately called Dr. Wall to schedule an appointment.

"Grace, I'm so happy to hear from you," the psychiatrist said, "and I eagerly look forward to seeing you—not just as a patient but as a friend and as a fan of yours. I'll move some things around on my schedule so I can make time to see you tomorrow morning, if that works for you. Does 10:30 sound good?"

Grace felt surrounded by so much love: the love of Ron, her children, Sally, and her newfound love of life. She also loved the clarity of where things stood in her life, which made the road before her seem free of obstacles. Now, with one more cup of coffee and two bagels, anything was possible.

A little while later, fully nourished, energized, and filled with enthusiasm, she descended to Ron's writer's garret and sat to write. She took a moment to appreciate how far she had traveled within her mind, heart, and soul. She looked heavenward and said, "Thank you, Jesus, for carrying me so far and getting me here."

She didn't notice the hours slip by, but Moonbeam certainly did. The feline had that "Hey, Mom, remember me?" look on her cute little mug as she stomped on the desk and onto the keyboard to type out her own two cents. Grace picked her up and draped her over a shoulder, stroking her over and over again in apology.

"Mommy is sorry, and she missed you too," she murmured.

Now that she had made her point, Moonbeam purred her forgiveness, albeit with an added "Don't let it happen again" warning to fill Mommy with guilt and dread. Grace had to accept that Moonbeam was her gal Friday. *Hmm, she deserves a mention on the acknowledgments page.*

Since part of Grace had fallen asleep already, she took Moonbeam's sage advice and decided to go upstairs and lie down—after feeding Moonbeam, of course—for a while before returning to her writing.

As she lay in bed, she realized she had indeed felt Ron's presence and guidance while writing, just as he said she would. She didn't hear him the way she did in her dreams; rather, when she sat and looked at the blank pages on her computer, she understood exactly how the book should proceed and how to end it.

Her strong sense of accomplishment and satisfaction had a sedative effect on her, helping her fall asleep almost instantly.

∼

She woke only because the grinning clock was laughing at her, loudly. Awake but not up, she put on the TV and found an old W. C. Fields movie to enjoy, watching it to the end. It was still funny. She knew where the most hilarious lines would happen and started laughing well before the scene appeared. Then she laughed even harder when the scene came on. Finally, she recognized that she was truly enjoying herself and the movie. *Maybe I have made it through the seven stages of grief. Maybe all that's left is that bittersweetness that stays with you.*

Grace didn't want to get back up. She rationalized that she wasn't being a bum by lounging in bed and enjoying her life again. Not only was this a necessary undertaking, but she was actually in a private writing conference with her story editor, Professor Moonbeam. And they had a lot to discuss and argue about.

Something that Ron had written popped into her head:

> *Writing won't let me sleep, and if I do sleep, writing will wake me up. It yells at me, loudly, to write it down before I forget it yet again.*

Now a writer herself, she realized how true that sentiment was.

She suddenly had an epiphany. She was hungry, which meant Moonbeam was doubly so. They toddled downstairs to see what was on today's menu in the refrigerator. Luckily, she found frozen tacos to heat up, which she did. She had officially become more "microwave compatible" in her culinary pursuits.

She sat in front of the TV and enjoyed her tacos. Maybe she would go back to writing today, and maybe she wouldn't. *Life is good! And it's getting "gooder."*

She ultimately decided to return to writing out of a sense of responsibility to Ron. She couldn't let her motivation stagnate. The writing itself wasn't difficult. It was a little like going on a long drive. It was good to stop occasionally to stretch your legs, along with the rest of you. But you had to get back on the road.

She also wanted to be able to tell Dr. Wall and Sally how much she had accomplished.

She drove her keyboard a little further along, closer to where she needed to be, maintaining the high quality of her writing. When the going got difficult, when the writing didn't flow as naturally as it should, she knew it was time to take another break; so she did. She and Moonbeam stretched out in bed once more, this time to watch a Marx Brothers movie, again gleeful at all the funny scenes to come.

Watching these old movies relaxed her. As she had hoped would happen at the very beginning of her mourning period, the classics made her feel more connected to Ron. Maybe Ron was also watching the movie, through Grace's eyes. Of course, these old movies were also really funny; why not enjoy that quality in and of itself? She was retired, free to do or to not do whatever she wanted to do or not do.

She did have another problem. Moonbeam the clock watcher frequently reminded her of the proximity to dinnertime by sitting on her chest.

"Down in front. Don't block the screen," Grace protested. *Can't the cat go to the refreshment stand like everyone else? Maybe an usher with a flashlight will escort this nuisance out, to the applause of the rest of the audience.*

Then again, maybe her only escape was to get back to writing. "Yeah, that's the ticket." At least with writing, she could be in a world she had created and could therefore control.

∾

Grace was up early for her appointment with Dr. Wall, who was eager to hear all she had to say. Dr. Wall greeted Grace warmly at her home office and suggested they start with a cup of tea. They both sat with cups in hand and gazed at each other momentarily.

Dr. Wall said, "There is something different about you, Grace. Something has changed—something significant."

"Sally said the same thing. What is it with me? Am I wearing the wrong color socks? Do they not match or something? Maybe it's the three new tattoos and my latest facial piercings; that's it, isn't it?" Grace quipped.

Dr. Wall chuckled. "Well, you're close. It's all of the above."

"Okay, I've got the message, Doc. After I leave here, I will go directly to Murray the photographer and try to see what you and Sally see."

"I hope he can photograph auras." The doctor smiled widely. "Why don't you tell me what's been happening in your life in the weeks since I last saw you?"

"Well, when I last saw you, I told you I was not ready or qualified to speak to your bereavement group. I didn't know if I was going through the mourning process correctly. I told Sally and my family I needed time to be completely alone. I felt that solitude was the best environment for self-reflection and most conducive for recognizing and going through the steps of grieving.

"Sally repeated something to me that Ron wrote in his tribute to his mother: that time takes time to work its wonders. And I think they were both right. She also suggested that I begin doing what I said I would do and go through Ron's unfinished writing projects and finish some of the books he started. Sally is incredibly wise. And I took her advice and began writing.

"I started by organizing and reviewing all the unfinished and incomplete writings in Ron's file cabinet. That took quite a while because mixed among manuscripts were random thoughts that filled me with joy and anguish to read, and also sweet notes, to me. It became a very emotional process. But I finally found three strong contenders for what I wanted to write.

"And that's when Ron returned to me in my dreams. He told me how pleased he was and suggested that other spirits or forces were also pleased I had started my own writing. Ron promised to help me and guide me. He told me I would feel his presence and guidance as I wrote. And I did. It's coming along nicely. And that has made a real difference in my life.

"As I said, Sally also noticed a significant change in me. She suggested that I see you and tell you about it. She feels that the changes in me might mean that somehow, through some amazing miracle, I have gone through all the stages, the full mourning process.

"Sally said that maybe because Ron comes to me in my dreams, it's like I haven't really lost my spouse; he's there to help me move on from him, in a way, which is so strange but so comforting, to have his approval. So, that is a major factor in making me different, she thinks. I don't know if that's true or even possible. Perhaps you could shed some light, Judith."

"Well, Grace, it is my professional opinion that Sally is not only absolutely correct but also absolutely brilliant. I had to go through years of schooling, training, and practice to arrive at the same conclusion a former Marine Corps drill instructor arrived at intuitively. Maybe I should ask her to join my practice, or at least do some consulting work."

Grace was pleased with this praise of her best friend but pressed, "Can you give me some clarification on how I could possibly pass through the seven stages and complete it so quickly, if I actually have?"

Judith replied, "That, my dear friend, is a great question. I wish I had a great answer for you. Hell if I know. But if you ever do figure out the answer, please let me know.

"The whole mourning and grieving process is mysterious and individual. Again, in my professional opinion, the whole process is certifiably *nuts*! It should be in a straitjacket in a padded cell. But somehow, it does work, eventually. I'm sorry that I can't explain it to you or to myself any better than that. I don't know how to explain your getting through all of the stages other than to say that it must be a genuine miracle. And you are writing, just as you said you would. You are a shining example for all of us, Grace. And you will be incredibly inspirational for my bereavement group when you feel the time is right to speak to them."

Grace held up a hand in the universal sign of "halt!" "Well, I've never had a miracle before. I have a lot to process right now. I do feel that I am closer to speaking with your bereavement group, but give me a little more time to get ready."

"That's great. You'll be fantastic, Grace. You should speak with Sally and see what she thinks. Then we'll go from there."

Grace suggested, "Well, maybe you can come over to my house, and you, Sally, and I can delve into this and come up with something. How about tomorrow at ten? Who knows, there may be some 'just baked, hot out of the oven' bagels in your future. And maybe you can speak with Sally about joining your practice."

"That sounds fantastic and delicious at the same time. I'll see you and Sally tomorrow at 10 a.m."

When Grace got home, she called Sally and invited her out to lunch. They went to Sally's favorite restaurant, sitting at a table outside with a great view of the ocean. They didn't need a menu. They knew what they wanted and ordered quickly. They began with a glass of wine each.

Sally started them off. "So, what are you waiting for? Are you the 'master of suspense'? Spill."

"Well, Sally, you may be getting an honorary degree from the 'University of Dr. Wall.' She thinks you're brilliant. She said she saw the same change in me that you had already seen . She may want you to join her practice; you're just so damn gifted. She fully agreed that I likely passed through the stages of grief. She doesn't know how it happened, only that she believes it did. She said it is a genuine miracle. So, I may be closer to speaking with her bereavement group than I thought, although I still have some serious doubts. She's coming by tomorrow morning to speak with both of us over some hot bagels."

Sally said, "Great, I'll bring the bagels, and you make the coffee. And it's my turn to agree with my esteemed colleague, Dr. Wall: I think you really did have a miracle, Grace."

After lunch, they enjoyed wiling away the day. They were just a couple of hot chicks on the beach, taking a stroll. Grace felt the time was right for the next part of her plan: surprising Sally by treating her to a day at the spa together as a thank-you. Sally was indeed surprised and even a little reluctant to accept Grace's gratitude, but Grace insisted that she wanted to get her friend "all dolled up" and glamorous for her meeting (interview) with her new business partner.

"All right, Grace. Let's not take this too far. I'm not really Dr. Wall's junior doctor in her practice. I am merely her senior consultant and resident guru for her really tough problems."

"Thank you so much for that illuminating clarification. We'll put some extra time aside tomorrow for us to meet with the sculptor so you can pose for your statue. I'll make sure he includes your golden halo in his completed work."

"That would be the perfect final touch, wouldn't it?"

The ensuing belly laughs almost made Sally's halo fall off her head.

~

After a wonderful day at the spa, it was time to head home. Grace pictured Moonbeam standing in the doorway, arms across her chest, one foot tapping on the floor. "Well, young lady, do you know what time it is? You could've called!" Grace laughed to herself as she walked inside. She would make something special for Moonbeam and then take a nap.

After Moonbeam's repast, they journeyed upstairs to cuddle each other to sleep. Moonbeam was teaching her to purr but was secretly afraid that her mommy was kinda dense and would never learn to do it properly. But hey, at least she tried.

Grace put on the boob tube and was gratified to find a station playing *The Little Rascals* again. The two companions slept contentedly until dinnertime.

They awoke to the darkness of night. *The Little Rascals* were long gone, and Madam Moonbeam was in a preemptive stare-down with Grace over dinner.

"Okay, okay. I'm heading for the 'royal kitchen' to prepare your 'royal meal,' my liege."

Grace bowed deeply as she backed out of the room so as not to offend Her Majesty.

When the royalty had been taken care of, the little people got the table scraps to feed themselves. Grace prepared (read: microwaved) something for herself.

As usual, she ate in front of the TV. Not that there was much to watch that was worthy of her time and attention. Luckily, Grace found a station playing *The Prisoner*, which would make her microwaved meal taste like a feast. And make Moonbeam purr with satisfaction.

CHAPTER 24

THE FRESH BAGEL CLUB

Grace woke up the following morning in bed, thoroughly confused. She thought and thought but could not figure out how Moonbeam had carried her upstairs. Apparently, there was no end to Moonbeam's magic.

She glanced at the clock.

"Oh my God, look at the time. I've got to get ready."

First, she took a quick shower in case Dr. Wall came over early. She could eat breakfast while getting dressed more easily than while showering. *Good call, Grace.* Not that she needed an appetizer for bagels. In fact, when she went to the kitchen window, she saw that Sally was on her way out to get breakfast.

About fifteen minutes before Dr. Wall was scheduled to arrive, Grace started the coffee machine. The house was pretty well straightened out. Everything was ready to go. She could gulp one more helping of coffee in peace before the doorbell rang.

Ding-dong, the doorbell sang. Dr. Wall was here. Grace hurried to welcome her.

Dr. Wall said, "My mom always told me to never arrive empty handed, so I couldn't help myself. I brought some danish."

"That's wonderful, Judith. We all love danish. Shall we sit in the kitchen or the living room? Where would you feel more comfortable?"

"Any place is fine for me, Grace."

"Okay, let's go to the kitchen. It's cozier. Sally went to get the 'hot out of the oven' bagels. She'll be back any minute now. There is milk, cream, sugar, anything you might like. Now, if I just gave you a cup of coffee, we'd be doing pretty well."

Grace told Dr. Wall about the day she and Sally had spent together after Grace left her appointment. The doctor listened with a big smile as her patient explained that she had wanted to show her undying gratitude and love for Sally. At the conclusion of that story, they heard the door open.

Grace yelled out, "We're in the kitchen, Sally."

"On my way." The delicious aroma from the bagels preceded her. A moment later, Sally appeared. She and Judith greeted each other like comrades in arms, each knowing and appreciating how the other was helping Grace.

Grace mentioned, "Judith brought some danish. She's one of those 'don't arrive empty handed' types."

"We're lucky to share those old-fashioned values. Means more food for everyone! Let's eat. I have a dozen fresh-baked bagels here. Name it and claim it."

The kitchen was a place for small talk and eating; serious talk would happen in the living room later. Sally went right for the blueberry bagel, Grace got the cinnamon raisin, and Judith grabbed the closest one, whatever the flavor. They all enjoyed the fresh bagels—just the thing to wash down their coffee. And they had a leisurely morning to eat them.

But eventually it was time to head for the living room to move ahead with the real purpose of the day.

They sat on three separate pieces of furniture in a semicircle. Dr. Wall began.

"Congratulations, Sally, for your spot-on diagnosis. I told Grace that you were brilliant in your intuitive assessment of the change we both saw in her. Perhaps we should consider working together somehow."

Sally replied, "Thank you, Dr. Wall, that is very flattering. But you and I can always find time to speak. Grace is of paramount importance here today. Let's try to keep the focus on her."

"You're right, of course. I just wanted to acknowledge your gifts and your contribution to helping Grace." Dr. Wall continued, "To that end, Grace, I believe you did pass through something very significant. Let's just call it a miracle because it is the only explanation that seems to fit the facts. As you say, since you still have occasional visits from Ron, you haven't entirely lost your spouse. Maybe that is the explanation.

"Most people haven't been as lucky as you are. Sally and I and the men and women of my bereavement group never got the miracle you did. And since you did receive that miracle, I believe you also acquired the responsibility to help other suffering people, such as those in my group. Would you be open to speaking with them in the near future, Grace?"

Grace said, "Judith, you're right. I believe that God has called on me to do this work. And I will do as God asks. In fact, I can speak with them at the next scheduled meeting."

Dr. Wall tried to rein in her enthusiasm to ask calmly, "We meet tomorrow, Grace. Can you be ready by then?"

After serious contemplation, Grace replied, "Not only can I do this, but I need to do this."

Dr. Wall was jubilant. "That's great, Grace. And, Sally, I would like you to come as well. You don't have to speak if you don't want to. But I think it will help Grace a great deal."

"Of course, Judith. I won't speak to the group, but I will be there for moral support for Grace and help in any way I can."

"Great, guys. We have a plan. The meeting will be tomorrow morning at eleven in the church basement. I'll see you there."

With her mission accomplished, Dr. Wall left to make the necessary arrangements and preparations for tomorrow's meeting.

Sally and Grace went to the kitchen to contemplate everything over more coffee and the surprise danish. As amazed as she was at Grace's progress, Sally was worried that her friend had undertaken a task beyond her current capabilities. *What will she say to the group? Does she even know? Is she planning to "wing it"? And most importantly, how can I help guide her and focus her to be ready for all she will face?*

Sally waited for Grace to speak.

However, Grace's mind was elsewhere. She remembered how to speak in front of a classroom of high school students as a music teacher; she simply had to put herself into the mindset that this was just another class to teach. *I'll think of what to say, and everything will go just fine*, she told herself.

Sally began, "Well, Grace, what is your plan? Do you need an outline you can follow? If not, should we work on one right now?"

"I don't know, Sally. I didn't have an outline when I gave Ron's eulogy. And everybody seemed to think that went well. Maybe I could do the same here."

Grace also couldn't help but think that if she'd had an outline at the funeral, she wouldn't have been able to wander and contemplate and make all the vital points she had realized in the moment. But perhaps the scenarios were different. She'd been afloat, untethered from solid ground following Ron's death. She was steadier now. Perhaps she needed to speak from that more unshakeable place.

Sally played the part of the logical voice in Grace's mind as she declared, "Grace, you need an outline to guide and focus your thoughts so you can make all the points to the group that you want to make. Shall we begin?"

Grace hesitated but then nodded.

Sally began, "First off, they've probably already heard some things about you. They've also probably been wondering about what they've heard about Ron's death. By your addressing that first, they will better know who you are and all you've been through. They will be able to sympathize with your loss and your suffering and relate to you as one of them. That will help them to focus their full attention on all you'll be saying. At that point, they're all yours."

"Sally, that's an excellent point," Grace agreed. "That would be the best way to start. I don't want their heads filled with unrelated questions. I'll let them all know who I am and why I am there. Then I can tell them about Ron and what he meant to me. I can tell them how my whole family suffered and how we helped each other cope. And of course, Sally, I'll tell them how you carried all of us through it and made everything work so smoothly.

"I think I've got it. I think I know where to take it from here. Thank you. Would it be okay to have breakfast at your house before heading to the church tomorrow? I think that would help me relax and focus on what I have to say and do."

Relieved, Sally placed her hand on Grace's on the table. "That would be perfect, Grace. See you mañana at my house for breakfast."

CHAPTER 25

BEREAVEMENT

Grace went over to Sally's house early the following morning. Her friend had made a large breakfast to sustain both of them through what would be a difficult day. Sally made a point of avoiding the subject of the speech. Instead, they discussed what she was playing in the kitchen. Joan Baez was singing one of Sally's favorite Bob Dylan songs, "You Ain't Going Nowhere." She especially loved the way Joan Baez sang it.

They got to Father Jerry's church half an hour early to collect their thoughts. Sitting on a bench outside the church, they reviewed the outline once more. When Grace felt fairly confident, they entered. Dr. Wall immediately came over to welcome them. She then led them to the basement where the meeting would soon begin. Grace and Sally sat in the audience area. Dr. Wall would call Grace up when it was time to speak. Sally held her friend's hand for moral support.

Dr. Wall began the regular weekly meeting of her bereavement group precisely at eleven.

"We have a very special guest today. She recently lost her husband in a tragic accident. I will let her tell you about herself and what she has been through. I think this will be a memorable meeting for all of us. Ladies and gentlemen, let me introduce an extraordinary woman whom I am proud to call my dear, dear friend, Mrs. Grace Butler.

Grace, would you please come up?"

Sally gave her friend a last supportive squeeze of the hand before Grace made her way to the stage.

She felt a little unsteady, but she grew steadier with each word.

"Ladies and gentlemen, despite what Dr. Wall has said about me, I feel wholly unqualified to speak to you today and downright inadequate. I feel like I should be in the audience, listening to each of you, to learn what I can from you. But Dr. Wall feels that I can make a significant contribution, so let me try.

"First off, let me tell you who I am and why I am here speaking with you. Like many of you, I am a patient of Dr. Wall. You may have heard that I recently lost my beloved husband, Ron Butler, in a tragic accident. Ron was the man who died in a drainage pipe not too long ago. The story was thoroughly covered in the newspapers and even more thoroughly and enthusiastically covered by all the gossips in the area. Not only did I lose the one true love of my life, but I lost him under circumstances that seemed to overshadow the wonderful life he lived and the amazing man he was.

"I'm sure that all of you already know that sometimes reality forces its way into your life, uninvited, tramples everything in its path, and hits you in the face with a two-by-four and a bucket of ice water. Then it pulls the rug out from under you and drops you hard, right on your ass.

"Ron was truly the sunshine on my face. We shared a love that defined a lifetime—make that two lifetimes. We both proved that the friendship, mutual respect, and love between two hearts is the firmest foundation on which to build a wonderful life together. Our love was our life. It was an incredible gift from God. We were blessed to have found each other. We completed each other. Now that my beloved husband has passed on, I am not only a new widow; I am incomplete. More of me is missing than remains.

"I spent a long while just orbiting my husband's grave in a slow-motion living suicide, unable to move on with my life. For the first time, God and I had *words*—sharp, angry, intentionally hurtful, blasphemous words fueled by so much pain, such intense, never-ending agony and suffering, with no possible end in sight. I said things to God that I never thought would pass my lips. Those words have been said and are now gone. But the intense, unremitting agony remains, undiminished.

"I can imagine how surprised you might be to hear me say this. Many of you have been in this same place from which I'm speaking. I am as alive as I can be without a heart. My heart died and was buried with him because I just couldn't stand the thoughts of our two hearts being separated.

"Now, you might wonder what Ron was doing in a drainpipe during the worst rainstorm and the heaviest winds in twenty-three years. Well, he went out looking for my cat, Moonbeam. He wanted to rescue her and get her back to the warmth and safety of our home, so when he heard a meow coming from that drainpipe, he crawled inside. He did that for me because he loved me so much.

"And he would have crawled out of the drainpipe if a massive tree hadn't fallen on him in all that rain and wind. Instead, my husband is dead.

"We've all heard the spiel. We all suffer and mourn in our individual, separate ways, on our own timetables. No two experiences are the same. And I myself have been a widow for a relatively short time. I'm still trying to figure all this out. I'm still trying to figure out how to avoid being 'stuck' in my personal, private hell for the rest of my life. I still worry about falling into some unbreakable pattern of mourning and suffering, stuck in a labyrinth of torment, unable to find a way out. I fear that I'm somehow still in the denial phase and haven't actually dealt with an ounce of my grief.

"I worry that even more severe depression will creep in like the brutal cold of winter finding its way into a closed room. Depression that will put me in a straitjacket of my own making. 'Here, put your arms in these nice, long sleeves; now give yourself a hug while we strap your arms in the back.' This is a burden I will have to work out for myself, or I will have to carry that burden for the rest of my life."

She fell silent for a moment before continuing. The room was utterly silent.

"I love music. I was a high school music teacher for many, many years. I even named my daughter Melody. Loving music as I do, I keep thinking of a lyric from the Gladys Knight and the Pips song 'Midnight Train to Georgia': 'I'd rather live in his world than live without him in mine.' I would rather have gone to heaven to be with Ron than continue here in my misery, living without Ron. I would rather have died than live without him. I mean that. Some of you may well have felt much the same at some point. Maybe you still do. The question is, how do I go on with my life and fulfill my life's mission and do God's work?

"I've been told that I have important things to do in my life. I have my children to live for. I am still their mother, now as a single parent. I can't afford to wallow in my self-pity. I have to be an example for my children. I have to get on with it.

"I can't get stuck in my life, digging the hole I'm in deeper and deeper. I can't be so selfish that I think only of myself, my pain. I will never be able to bring Ron back to life, to make things as wonderful as they once were. That would be like putting raindrops back in the clouds after a rainstorm. So, I decided I need a purpose.

"My beloved husband was a gifted and successful writer. Some of you may have heard of him; you might even have read his books. Ron named our son, Ryder, as a tribute to his love of writing. Our son is studying to become a writer like his father. At Ron's funeral, I told everyone that I thought the best way to honor Ron was to begin writing myself. I proofread all of Ron's books for years. I think I know his style quite well. I am working to finish some of the story ideas Ron started on but hadn't completed. The books are in Ron's style but with the tender addition of my own style and my approach to his work. I don't know if Ron's legions of fans will accept me. But I think that this will help me. And maybe I'm being selfish, but I need to help *me* right now. By writing, I am turning my pain into literature.

"I am now well underway in writing and completing that first book. There are several more books I plan to work on in the near future. By writing, I am turning my pain into literature. Maybe I'm lucky to be able to have a plan. I hope all of you have some idea of what you want to do with your own lives. That is entirely up to you. But for me, writing is how I prevent myself from getting stuck. It is how I can escape the agony I feel twenty-four seven. And it is a way to honor the incredible true love that Ron and I are still blessed to share.

"This is what I will be doing with my life. I believe everything is possible when you learn to accept that you don't need to know and understand everything and you don't need to control everything. Only then can you accept things as they are. I believe that I have evolved to a place where I can accept things in the world and in my life, without needing to control them. I have become an 'accepter.'

"I don't need to know how a magician performs his magic. Intellectually, I know it is a trick. But the delight of magic lies in the mystery, the amazement, and the wonder. I don't need to know how love performs its miracles. I'm simply grateful that there is love. I don't know the process by which love becomes 'in love.' But I'm glad that it does and that love was able to work its amazing miracles for my late husband and me. Love is a gift to us from God. Love comes from God. Ron is with God. So, for me, Ron is love!

"Speaking of love reminds me of one of my many favorite quotes from Albert Einstein. He said, 'Gravity is not responsible for people falling in love.' And I can't help but think about some of the things my husband wrote. He wrote some lovely, very romantic thoughts about me that were never published. Some he wrote for Valentine's Day, some for my birthday and other occasions. He wrote, 'Your beauty shines like winter's sun through the purest crystal.' He also wrote, 'I didn't try to find a place in my heart for love. I tried to find a place in love's heart for me, for us.' The last one is 'We are old soulmates from a previous reincarnation, reunited in this life, by the grace of

God.' Those are some of my all-time favorites. They've made me cry every time, thinking about how loving they are."

The emotions overwhelmed her momentarily with more tears, painful in their saltiness.

"What can we say about love that poets and singers haven't already best expressed? So many love songs are about him, about us. For me, love is benevolent madness, but madness nevertheless. When you're in love, you're a paranoid optimist. Go figure that one out."

She continued, "I recall when my husband got me a beautiful gift. I thanked him, but I asked about the occasion. What was the reason? He said, 'I got it because I love you.' 'But there is usually a reason for getting a gift,' I protested. He answered so lovingly, 'No reason. Love *is* the reason.' That is the kind of love I'm mourning. That is why I'm in such intense pain.

"But despite that pain, I feel I have somehow emerged on the other side of a tunnel."

Her captive audience sensed a turn in her tone here. A few straightened in their seats. Sally gave Grace an encouraging smile.

"I've had some strange experiences following my husband's death. And I've learned life lessons I could not have learned any other way than in the way I did. This will probably sound mysterious, magical, mystical, and totally *nuts* all at the same time.

"The most important thing I've learned is that love does not end; life ends, but love transcends life. Love transcends death. It advances to a much higher level of loving. My husband's death was not the end of our love. That higher level is still attainable for us. I know this to be true because I've experienced it myself, more than once. My late beloved husband has come to me several times in my dreams.

"How can I try to explain that process to you? Well, I'm sure everyone here remembers the Beatle's song 'Let It Be.' Paul McCartney wrote it after his late mother, Mary, came to him in a dream. She wanted to reassure her son that everything would be all right and he should just 'let it be.' For me, my husband brought me this message. I know that sounds like a vivid dream, an illusion, self-deception, wishful thinking, etc. But for me, it was a life-changing, lifesaving experience. It certainly changed my life for the better. It made it possible for me to speak with you today, so recently after my husband died. How is that possible? I don't know, and I don't need to know. I accept it.

"I believe it is a miracle. Ron has helped and advised me. He has given me the strength, the courage, and the words to be here today. He gave me the words to fulfill the purpose I found for myself and the purpose God has given me. For me, that is unquestionably a *miracle*!

"I know that love goes on, because my love has in fact gone on; and it will continue for the rest of my days on earth. And I am beginning the process of restarting my life. I am seeking 'rebirth' after death, Ron's death. God has given me the wisdom to know this and to live it. My late husband and I will continue to share this incredible love until and far beyond when we are reunited, when God wills it.

"I think of Ron throughout the day, every day. And I think of what my life is now and what the future may hold for me. I think about how to be a better, more loving mother for my fatherless children. When Ron died, my life was filled with despair and many uncertainties, but especially the loss of hope. The only rest I could find was on my 'bed of nails,' crying a flood of tears, suffering constantly. I felt so powerless. I didn't feel like I had control over where my life was going. In a deep hole of depression, I wanted to give up responsibility for myself and for others, even my loved ones.

"Ron's death was a sudden vacuum, in his own words—the Great Eclipse in my life. This sudden vacuum is what unites us here, as a group, in our common struggle. I don't have to tell any of you about grief and mourning. Who knows it better than you? You live with it the same as me. I had a lot of survivor's guilt. Dear God, why am I not dead too? Is this some kind of test or some trial to test my loyalty, my morality, to test my love?

"I still suffer from lack of an answer. When you're adrift, you don't particularly care what happens. You go where the tide takes you, wherever that may be. 'Where the tide takes me is not my responsibility; it's the tide's responsibility. Whatever happens to me happens. After all, I am the victim here.'

"I don't know about you folks, but I had to ask myself for permission to get out of that hole of depression and despair. Would I be betraying the love Ron and I shared if I did? How can I go on with my life when Ron cannot go on with his—when Ron cannot go on being the amazing husband and fantastic father he always was, because he is dead? But these questions brought up a new one: can I still go on being an incredible mother? Of course I can. I have to. I'm all they've got. By honoring our children, I honor the love Ron and I shared and the children we raised together. And that is doing God's work.

"I have chosen to find new hope and purpose in my life through my children and by writing, as a way of honoring Ron and the true love we shared. Each of us, as individuals, hopefully will seek and discover our own ladder by which to climb out of the hole each of us is stuck in. Some may find the depression familiar, even comfortable, because they have adjusted to that predictable life. I believe the first step to getting out of that hole is to simply *choose to do so*! It sounds too simple to be true, but it is true. It's your voluntary prison. You can leave whenever you decide to leave.

"You will discover that your choice to get out *is* the ladder. Past the ladder, you will see the light. The light will illuminate your way to a door. Going through that door is how you restart your life.

"The process is not easy, but it is straightforward. At least, that is the process that has worked for me so far. Some individuals may feel stuck with their survivor's guilt, like they have to continue in their 'righteous suffering' as an expression of their eternal love. Perhaps they fear finding hope. What can be worse than that? My wish is that someday they will receive hope joyously and find new purpose and rejoin the world and all the people who have loved them and missed them and who have been waiting for them so very long.

"I used to have a life; then I had death, Ron's death. Now I have discovered a new life. To enter it, I have to be reborn, reincarnated. Perhaps you folks need to do the same. I'm sure we all want to get back to having a life again. If you don't choose it, it will never happen. You can't be made to do it, not even by God. You yourselves have to make the choice, for you and your families. I am living proof that such a change can happen—if you do the work with the guidance of Dr. Wall and the support of all those who love you and want to care for you.

"I don't know if I've said what I was expected to say today or if I said what was required of me. I just spoke from the heart; and I hope I made sense to somebody, or at least gave comfort or created room for thought or motivation. As individuals, we are all different. But some things in life make us all feel pretty similar. And I think the death of a loved one qualifies.

"There is one final thought I want to leave with you today. I firmly believe that among all the incredible gifts God's love gives us, the greatest is that you can give so much love away and still have it all.

"Thank you all for listening to me. God bless each and every one of you. Thank you. Softly into silence, I leave you."

With her presentation completed, Grace went to Sally, who took her hand. Many in the group, both men and women, were crying; many seemed almost bewildered. Some of them felt that they just witnessed a miracle. They were left with much to process, much to consider. Each individual felt in their hearts that Grace was speaking directly to them and them alone. Truly touched, the entire group stood in unison in a silent standing ovation, a salute to Grace and an acknowledgment that something quite meaningful had just happened—something they would always remember.

Dr. Wall felt like her script had been ripped into tiny pieces and tossed into the air. As the self-appointed president of Grace's fan club, as Judith, she was cheering wildly inside, but as Dr. Wall, the psychiatrist for the group, she struggled to figure out just what to do or say next.

Dr. Wall went to the stage thinking, *How do I follow that presentation and bring everyone back down to earth?*

She finally asked, "Does anybody have any questions? Anyone?"

∼

The coffee and bagels were on Sally today as they headed home. She wore a proud smile as she pictured Grace autographing books for her legions of fans.

In the car, Grace mentioned, "You know, Sally, it's curious that I haven't seen Angela in a while. And I haven't seen Ron much recently. I wonder what that means."

Sally answered with a light shrug, "Maybe it means you graduated. Maybe you've grown beyond the need for Angela. But remember, Grace, you and your 'muse,' Ron, will be working together on your books. After all, you're his official ghostwriter. And I feel that he will be near when you need him." With a grin, she added, "But you'll be the one autographing the books."

THE END

www.ingramcontent.com/pod-product-compliance
Lightning Source LLC
LaVergne TN
LVHW041841070526
838199LV00045BA/1387